Johnny Dolphin

Johnny Dolphin was born in Western Oklahoma in 1929. He is a poet-playwright-novelist, an engineer-ecologist, an entrepreneurial manager, and a philosopher of systems theory. From 1949–1952 he published his first book of poems, THE DREAM AND DRINK OF FREEDOM, made his living as a fruit picker in the Western states, and then as a factory worker in Chicago where he engaged in organizing and strengthening unions. Serving as a machinist with the US Army Engineers in 1952 he became interested in engineering systems, and in 1953 entered the Colorado School of Mines on the G.I. Bill of Rights, graduating with Honors and as President of the student body in 1957. From 1960–62 he studied at Harvard Business School graduating with distinction as a Baker Scholar.

As mining-metallurgical engineer he headed a special metals group for Allegheny-Ludlum, an Uranium crushing leaching 1000 tpd plant for UCNC, then after Harvard Business School worked on Regional Development Projects in Iran and W. Africa for David Lilienthal's Development Resources Corp., ran a million square mile coal exploration program, and was President of two independent corporations.

In November of 1963, Johnny Dolphin abandoned the New York entrepreneurial-engineering stage to make a two-and-a-half year journey around the planet, living with the Avant-garde and Berbers in Tangiers, Morocco, then as an Arab across N. Africa, then living with tribal chiefs and Shaman from Malakal on south in the Sudan, and continuing east to India, Nepal, Vietnam and Japan on the open road studying the traditional cultures, philosophies, and history of Civilizations on the planet.

Returning to the States, Dolphin co-founded the Caravan of Dreams Touring Theater in 1967 for which he has adapted some thirty plays, co-founded the Institute of Ecotechnics in 1973, gives poetry readings, lectures in the theory of advanced systems, and consults on entrepreneurial enterprises based on collegial management and ecotechnic principles. His publications include THE COLLECTED WORKS OF THE CARAVAN OF DREAMS THEATER, VOL. I & II. His book SUCCEED, STRUCTURING MANAGERIAL THOUGHT is soon to be published by Synergetic Press.

312 Houston St., Fort Worth, Texas
24 Old Gloucester Street, London

ISBN No. 0 907791 07 7

Cover design by BERTOLD WOLPE
Cover illustration by GERALD WILDE
"The Rope Dancer", reprinted with special permission. Wilde's work on permanent exhibition at The October Gallery, London.
Typesetting by CECILIA BOGGIS
Printed by EXPRESS LITHO SERVICE (OXFORD)

Johnny Dolphin

39 Blows on a gone Trumpet

"An American Escape Story"

SYNERGETIC PRESS

1

I grinned when my buddy, Bill Layton, accelerated to miss the stop light crossing the Bowery. "Why do you let them bother you? You don't owe them anything just because they wipe your windshield."

Sometimes I strode downtown from my medium rise Village apartment, caught my hot coffee and scrambled eggs from the pert pretty Black waitress in the efficient stainless restaurant on Broadway, thought of the latest chick snoozing under my sheets, always a swinger, sometimes a conversationalist, logically reviewed a presentation for the 9:30 meeting on the irrigation development in Iran, not forgetting to enjoy the decaying texts and textures on the gravestones by blackened Trinity Church, to glance down Wall Street, recall the dynamite pocks on the Morgan building, anarchic warning before World War I to unaware holders of power, then deploy during the 9:30 meeting the latest group dynamics I'd dug at the special Harvard course, in the worst case ready to adjust my viewpoint to the majority, remembering that sometimes a man has to lose in the short run to gain his soul in the marathon, also that nothing human is predictable, that even Caesar lost battles and finally his life, then after the meeting, a quick walk to the Heliport, the rotor whirl over wharfs, millions, offices, factories, superhighways, neighborhoods, suburbs, to the Boeing 707 jet with slim waitresses that deposited me, lunched and refreshed by Yogi breathing, in Denver by 1:00pm, when I strode to the Hertz rent-a-car, produced my charge card, two minutes later accelerated a new Chevrolet toward the mountains, a stop in Golden to pick up the geologist, and over the Divide devoured a thick steak at 6:30pm, and later that night working out a new theory of coal seam formation in ten thousand square miles of cretaceous sandstones.

Too bad the millions toiled, mired in misery, apathy, or comfort, predictable in their response to within one percent by any careful poll of opinion. But then Plato had his slaves, the Medici their artisans, the English their peasants and colonies—when had it ever been different? Did Haroun Al-Rashid's splendour provide more than dreams to his masses? And surely Hollywood, the Churches, Science, Press, offered any dream a mass-particle might desire?

No, pity was the vice of Christians, the slave disease, the weapon by which the many induced the few to die by their own hand.

No, only Energy or Will or Power or Creativity or Surge. I loved New York, loved life, was thirty-two and the world seemed at my feet.

2

In the kitchen 'everybody' (family 'everybody') struggling to keep down a thick slab of red meat, finally shoving it in an ice cube freezing pan and sliding a metal lid over it. However, instead of stowing this into the icebox, they (and 'they gradually became 'we') placed it over an open flame on the stove.

The raw living writhing meat convulsed in its prison; we kept sliding the metal lid back to see if life had left, but it convulsed ever more energy. It seemed evil, destructive, fascinating, at times turning into an eel, or a moray.

My fingers and yet not my fingers pushed it down whenever it tried to escape. The meat pulsed, vibrated, scorched my fingers. Finally I broke from the house and ran round the block. All the houses looked alike, the lawns all neatly mowed.

After almost around the block, I passed a man smoking a pipe on his front steps, chuckling. "I started all this," the man said, "I started all this cutting down."

Only two houses from home. The grass around the house next to mine, unkempt, full of weeds. Felt my own lawn would be even more confused.

Flung myself down on the curb and saw father and brother strolling around the side of the house. I pointed a rifle at them.

"Now I know what you really think of us," father shouted and he and brother disappeared inside the house, carelessly turning their backs on me and rifle.

I ran inside to join them and the struggle with the writhing menacing hunk of meat flared anew. Somebody hefted butcher knife and cleaved off a piece that continued writhing on the floor. Panic took everyone—whether to keep chopping up the huge hunk into many small writhings or keep trying to hold it down.

Somebody turned on hot water to flush the hunk down the drain but a yellow chicken claw already stopped the drain and everyone feared to slide back the metal top too far. They kept opening the freezing pan a little way, then slamming the top shut. The meat screamed, "Let me out, let me out, and I'll destroy you all."

3 Rufus Brown's secretary, looking cool and unfucked, wrinkled her nose and forehead at me in my office doorway, wiggled a shoulder, and made exclamatory jerks with her left hand. Rufus wanted to see me on the Iran project! Congratulations to myself so intuitive aware always sizing up secret totem messages wigwagged a million nonverbal ways under the fluorescent calm that even when new seemed ancient, an archaeological excavation with all passion's shouts echoed down and all flesh rotted.

Gradually sat up from lounging thought, stood and moved long legs down the office manfully retaining my clodhopper stride (so enthusiastic!) though all the rhythms pulled at my feet to break arc six inches before completing stride—what the hell, I had strength to bulldoze all tensions into flat raceway where exultation's scream's enough glory for all the sweat and training and even loss so long as the race exciting.

Rufus "explored" with long pauses between words and phrases his thoughts, carefully fitting them to an actuality he knew too complex but which he knew someone would be fitting words to and believing he at least knew his deficiencies whereas some others didn't fell to with good conscience though even that wintry sun doubt-beclouded.

"We have often felt," he began directly, "that we should have a thorough study made of our overall managements, but we feel our methods have been evolved from a special experience that many academic minds, or minds trained in conventional business, cannot appreciate. You, who have just begun with us, fresh from your Harvard training and your somewhat unusual past, might well be able to combine an objectivity with a perception of what we're trying to do."

Rufus put his hands together and gazed out over the Hudson toward the Jersey palisades. Is he really seeing anything? I remembered Rufus, high, flushed, good-humored, with highball in hand at company party in his high Manhattan apartment with balcony and fine mahogany table loaded with hors d'oeuvres and drinks, Rufus saying, "Faulkner said men between twenty and forty have no compassion. I've often wondered if men ever have compassion," and wandering on to others to talk briefly and to listen.

Rufus turned back to gaze at me, almost in surprise, I felt, that anyone in his office. "You must realize it took a lot of thought, to decide to take on the Iran job. It looks like a pattern now, because we like to make patterns out of the things we do, but in the beginning, six years ago, we took one small step and then another–"

The maps of the project huge, the size for military campaigns. Rivers, mountains, towns, forests, canals, roads, railway, crop patterns, rainfall, all written out in that most artistic of all factual communications, the map. Pulling out the great maps, pouring over them (actually scanning them, picking out this and that, but trying to pore over them, sweat pouring out, hot sun, midday, couriers, "General, what next?"), and feeling every more awed at size of the project. 718,334 acres to be irrigated from a 476-foot thin double-arch dam that would give a regulated flow of 1086 cfs, and thereby also stopping floods, and raise the per capita income of 58,900 peasants in 203 villages from $38 to $104 per annum not including side benefits of better health, better supervision of landowners' dealings with peasants, and soil conservation. "Even more," Rufus pointed out, in the first annual project report, "the faith of the people of Iran will be increased in the power of their co-operative action to secure more and better food and other amenities, and in fact this faith and the decision of Your Excellency are at the cornerstones of this project."

What was running a mine, or running after a girl, or being a coffee-drinker, compared to this elation of making history? An old canal of the Edomites, plugged-up by Tamurlane, being re-used. A country tugged (as some reporters would say) this and that way by the conflicting pulls of Soviet pressure and American example being influenced in its very guts by practical action programs.

"Action," Rufus mused, "we could not afford to become involved in only paperwork. We had to feel commitment to action program or we could not participate."

Like a boy who's kissed a girl's mouth, a neck, felt one or two breasts, several shoulders, many hands, an occasional knee, and cannot say what any of this means, knows all this by itself nothing, and yet necessary to come to grips with the main thing, so these maps, Rufus, my economic books, my talks with returned engineers all made special music in my glamour-struck-starved-seeking because knew one day soon I'd board a plane, fly to Iran, and there involve myself by decisive union with history.

4

Long continuous seats molded green plastic facing each other. Roaring, rattling, accelerating, stopping, cargoes of people hurtled somewhere. Blackened, grimy, glasses and beards scrawled on advertising's pretty girls, and toilet obscenities also for these transportation flisholes.

I notice her when I boarded the car at Fourth Street. Golden, golden blond, tanned, hair close to her temples almost white from the sun, eyes wide apart, blue, snub nose thick full lips, strong arms and legs like you'd grab flesh instead of flab, air of vitality and innocence. High heels, simple dress, sheer stockings. Hair combed very glossy. A perfect Wellesley type, I decided, wanting to be able to pick out every representative American at a glance.

Probably taking off between her junior and senior years and looking for a little excitement in New York for the summer.

She looked at me occasionally and I began trying to put meaning into my glances. She didn't leave Penn Station or Times Square. Excited. Impossible that she'd get off at 86th Street. Began to hope. Cool and tanned, she hardly sweated in the June subway heat. The tired, weary, lined, battered faces of general humanity subway cut out. I focused only on this vibrant, elegant girl. Never expect anything, an old voice warned inside, but damn it I did expect—what? Something unusual, intense, charged.

We both rose just before the train stopped at 86th. "How do you like New York? You're from Wellesley, aren't you?" Our eyes laughed at each other. "No, no," she said, and that disposed of Wellesley.

The push of disgorging people seemed to be lifting us up the stairs. Hardly conscious of my own legs moving.

"Nice talking to you, I go on to 90th." I shook her hand, felt skin, saw glints of gold blue, brown, kaleidoscoped inside, and wheeled away.

Reaching the West side of Broadway, stopped, turned. There. There she walked, disappearing, disappearing, nameless, unknown, twig down the river, death, gold into grime, she into them, you into it, the cars, stoplights cut me off like a canyon, no shout could reach, no signal, not to be endured, hollow and fire from chest to pelvis, fingers sliding off glass. No!

Found myself running, dashing across Broadway, dodging cars, to the green in the middle, Goddam truck, dash again, pardon me, her elbow in my hand, her elbow in my hand.

Her eyes, her eyes blaze. "I thought how stupid it'd be for you to leave and I never know how to reach you–" Silence. "I want to talk to you more!"

"I'm leaving for Puerto Rico in three days, but call me at this number. A friend of mine might be interested in meeting you." She broke open her purse and wrote out in huge letters, LUCY MORELAND OL 6–5138.

The skin between her fingernail and knuckle whitened from the decisive grip on her pen. People flowed by us like wind round a tree. "I'll call you."

"I'll be home after six."

"Goodbye." Folded a little slip of torn paper and slipped it into inner coat pocket.

After re-crossing Broadway, I turned again. She bobbed out of sight, but this time the tides would bring her back, would cast her on my beach, or I might swim after and join her. Did not go immediately to visit my friend in the tall apartment house on West End Avenue, but descended into the green almost tropically lush vegetation growing on the concrete slabs upthrust by steel to make a park over railroad tracks.

5

I cringed when Bill Layton tried so hard to miss the stoplight crossing the Bowery. I always walked past bums without giving anything, but tried to do it coolly not make any special try. One simply had to think hopeless, how could anyone help anything by picking random A from collection X to help when this obviously doesn't help everyone in collection X and therefore unjust to help A since one can't help everyone—if more people only knew how to operate simple logic no A would ever be unjustly helped—and besides why should A get my money just because I can afford some? Why couldn't Bill drive blithely by ignoring the men hustling from the curb to dab at a windshield? Life full of crises. A man, a healthy man, absolutely can't take on the burden of others, it'd crack him up, and besides be crucified or hemlocked by those he tried to help.

Poor Harlem Blacks , ha! The A-trainers, drunk sleazy, arrogant, because making out with plump guilty Bronx bagel babies, thought every white chick fair game at Washington Square fountain and more forward than Neapolitan Italians paraded their legendary prowess that they as well as projecting whites now believed no matter how drunk or undernourished or sawed-off.

Puerto Ricans lipstick loud and smeared and can't those girls ever realize they caricature the worst of Hollywood and are just too much?

Soot at the end of the day, soft, smudgy layer on my skin that peeled from a wettened neck by a fingernail could write smeary words. Noise, honking, jackhammer, bus exhaust, truck gear, heel-clicking, radio deep rounded patient persistent relentless ruthless voice noise, commercial TV noise, TV melodramatic noise, scratchy record noise, yes, I can hear some music above the scratches, quite good Dada, and clean-up boys rattling trays of dishes and silverware for all us swine feeding efficiently at trough long as we give up our money porkchops to our farmers, good loud movie noise drowning out all other noises except screams sometimes from the apartment building behind when I sat at movie's balcony's back, the subway roaring shake, and the talking of all the people repeating misunderstood script or what Mary said last night—NOISE!

I hated New York as nothing no person no place ever before. Waiting for subways, automatic elevators, taxis, waiters, raw winter to end, muggy summer to vanish, paydays to pay, Friday nights, Saturday nights, new girls, new assignments, new books, new plays, new records, new insights, new wit, new dishes of food, new clothes, new old neighborhoods, new movies, new reruns of old movies, the new *Times,* the new *Village Voice*, the new old *Realist* copies, for the rush to end, for the grind to grind down, for the lease to end, for the diamond needle to wear out, for the elbows in my tweed coat to wear out and then apply patches, for life to begin, for death to come, for new miracles, new erections, new memories of old sloshing realized potencies—WAITING!

Reading. I read and read and read. One particularly mad week in July I read Thomas Wolfe's *Web and the Rock* (second time), Durrell's *Clea*, Henry Miller's *Time of the Assassins*, Albee's *Zoo Story* (after seeing the play), 8 chapters of Keinkle's *Tropical Africa*, a translation of Yevtushenko's poems, and a collection of Stevenson's *Speeches.* In addition, I'd read five daily and one Sunday *New York Times*, all the bottom of page 17 news about what was *really* happening in

Cuba and South Vietnam, and not forgetting to follow Willie Mays in the back sports pages, a copy of the *New York Post* on Monday afternoon, the *World-Telegram* on Tuesday, Wednesday resisted the temptation, also Thursday, but by Friday had to check up on Hearst and read the *Journal American*, plus throwing down a what-the-hell 10¢ for the *Enquirer* which featured a particularly interesting story of a mother cutting up her sons, and, of course, the *Village Voice* from cover-to-cover including advertisements, noting with regret Jane Kramer's quitting to write for the *New Yorker*, and especially reading Jonas Mekas on new movies. Then there had been looks at *Fortune Magazine* (for big business viewpoint), at *Time* (for whitecollar propaganda shit), at *Life* (for the line pushed out to the masses and the amoebic intelligences devouring anything), at the *National Review* (right wing viewpoint), the *Reporter* (middle-of-road viewpoint), the *Nation* (pseudo-left viewpoint but too much effort to get the *Guardian* this week), *Vogue* article on women's fashions, Norman Mailer in *Esquire*, Nelson Algren in *Playboy* or was it Herbert Gold?, innumerable advertising posters, neon signs, the menu at least six times at the *Hip Bagel*, at least six other menus, labels on 4 beer bottles, the vitamin information on my box of Bran Flakes, the movie bill of coming attractive classic movie re-runs at the Bleecker, snatches of the *Kama Sutra* (someday I'll finally finish it) and W.H. Auden and Castro's speech before Batista's court at the Sheridan Square Bookstore waiting for a date, references in the *Handbook of Physics and Chemistry*, one word (Mandala) in the *Unabridged*, letters from Mother, from Phil, from Fran, from my bank, from the *Village Voice* (advertising questionnaire, please fill out), and from the electric company. Plus two company project reports, fifteen company letters, and the production statistics on the Iranian project illustrating need for and effect of nitrogen on sugar cane in the Khuzestan. And the subtitles on Antonioni's *l'Eclipse*—Reading!

The unexamined life is not worthy living. The examined life has been unworthy of living. Take a deep breath, brisk walk, reflect on Greek death poetry and mathematics, think of freezing on mountain climbs, drowning in oceans, how to turn a knife in your belly, remember tomorrow has always, so far, come, and the senseless joy spring and frolic forth and when health burbles and bubbles can rationalization, even meaning, be far behind?

6

How in the glitter and the void, on this revolving rotating wobbling spheroid cored with fused metals, skinned with sea and wrinkling mud, swirling a tugging robe of air, among peoples, cities, prairies, mountains, deserts, jungles, time past to first explosion and time future when all freezes to monotony, and amongst surging psychic intervals, bounces, thrusts, how could I feel certain that someday Lucy and I would rendezvous and that must take place if I'm to know what I must know?

Yet I felt certain even when hurrying to her Brooklyn Heights apartment, strewn with clothes, furniture, food, gadgets, her ceaseless motions, found her almost packed for Puerto Rico. Even when she said, "This is Fran," and I felt elation at Fran's appearance. Knew still that Lucy and I would have a rendezvous.

"Go on, get out, you two," Lucy cried, intent on stuffing her suitcase full. "Landau will be here any minute to say goodbye and I don't want you two around."

"Okay," I laughed, joyous from the warmth of her apartment, her excited packing, and tall lean Fran whose eyes moved with my face. "See you when you return."

I took Fran's hand and our palms sought full against each other. Down the steps, skipping along the street. Small, then great arcing ground-covering skips. We stopped and laughed.

"You're different than I thought," Fran said.

"How, how?" Always curious what people thought of me. Who isn't? Yes, sure of what I thought of myself, never really caring, but then perhaps because too spoiled—what if several in a row thought bad?

"I thought you'd be—dignified, or something. You're thirty-two and you have a responsible job, you know, but you're young—young—young."

"Is that good?"

"Yes!"

Youth always good, who against youth, why had I stayed this way, no become more this way, I who'd been so ancient-wise from since I could remember. Death, always conscious of death, each day the fates spared me death or mutiliation, somehow the ever more statistically improbable blood and potency sang sweeter. And this I expressed to her in broken urgent rhythms, words, glances, hand pressings and fingertwinings.

Fran turned out to be nineteen. "I thought you were twenty-one!" Oh, we played the scale of ages. Why did she have to say I younger than I was, I she older than she was? Age, sex, class, region, two mortal liquid-filled sacs—all set us apart, but something pulled us together. Age, first we smoothed down that difference. Why smooth down differences? I wanted her. Did she want me? What else? Reductionalist, I heard Ben Jefferson crying flapping green army-jacketed arms as we paced around and around the campus finally to sink exhausted onto the coffeehouse chairs and there continue our talk sometimes ending eight hours later standing shivering foot-stamping dead-tired half-angry half-exultant under fall and winter skies, achingly brittle leaves or transient snow, he puff puff snorting on his pipe nearly always out of fire. The world is multi-leveled, chemistry is not explained by physics, biology by chemistry, society by biology, nor the individual by society. Fran and I had to work out the levels, approach, recoil, approach.

Her candle worth the game. Spray moistened our faces on the ferry stern. I stood behind her narrow deep buttocks cleaving into my midriff. Later, when all was over, she told me, "It was the first time any boy had seized my hand on being introduced. But I certainly wasn't going to pull it away."

Somehow talked to her. "I wanted to know everything. I studied engineering law, history, anthropology. I wanted to act in the action. So I would never teach or write. I run projects. I union organized, wandered the West, went to three universities and ran a mine out on the Western Slope and now I work on projects to develop underdeveloped areas.

"I wanted to know every kind of American. Someday maybe I will be President. I wanted to know how this country is really built, how steel is made, how cars are formed, how wheat's grown, how cattle are slaughtered and peas frozen, how schoolbooks are written and paintings painted, how different kinds of girls make love, how pay-offs are slipped to cops, sentences meted out, cancers diagnosed, corporations financed, unions organized, candidates nominated, voting booths policed, advertisements concocted, professors appointed and what psychoanalysts hear."

"And did you do all this?"

"Most of it."

"What different kinds of girls?"

"Whore to Boston debutante."

"I was a debutante in New York."

"I don't hold it against you."

She laughed. "I never heard that before."

"I don't. I think even individuals of the upper class can be OK. Can rise above their environment. Same way as the exceptional slum kid." I laughed, now, but serious, too. Image: the classless Westerner, my jeep bounced over Grandfather's ranch in Western Indian State and I faced down blizzard and sand storm. Pitied those born into slums, the middle class, the upper class. In the West, the dying, already dead West men were men, Oscar Wilde won plaudits for his carnations, poodle, and wit, states and constitutions gained formulation, mountains yielded riches to shafts and tunnels, prairies billowed wheat, every individual went to hell in his own way, and Mark Twain composed epics. All in the day's work for a Joe Madison. Naturally, I could be tolerant of class-foibled East where young men aped their fathers or else fathers of those richer than themselves.

Coming back, we sneaked onto the top deck of the ferry. "See, those lights. Why does no one ever speak of Jersey City's lights. Manhattan's lights, poetry. Jersey City's lights, garbage dumps. Why?"

Her hair blew against my face. I kissed her. "Keep talking," she said. I kissed her again and her lips responded. "I liked it better when you were talking." I didn't believe her, but began to talk, feeling her buttocks sway press against me. I had never known a smart, rich, good-looking girl of nineteen. I wanted Fran Marble. Yet no direct sexual thoughts flashed. A battle of souls. I had to win her. "Come down and see me next weekend," I said.

"All right."

7

She didn't come. A letter arrived, incoherent, full of interesting phrases. But she wasn't coming. At the bottom she said I could write care of her grandparents at Gravel's Point, Long Island.

I called. "Fran. Why aren't you coming?"

"I can't. I've promised my folks that I'm going to study hard until I graduate. You know you wouldn't be good for that."

"People can't set time limits on every stage of life. If something happens, they can't ignore it." I spoke urgently into the receiver as if she were only an inch away. Hated the man lounging outside the booth, acting very bored and impatient—trying to provoke my conscience to finish my call.

"It just won't work. You're too different from all I've ever known."

"If our two worlds could join—what a world that would make!" Line or truth, wit or profundity, who could tell? I wanted to see her again, had to see her again, all words were lies all words some truth, so I could use any, if promised help attaining object, because that was true, I wanted her—at least wanted to see her, to love her once, twice, did really want her like forever? No, but that didn't diminish wanting her now.

"Why don't you come out here for a weekend, then?" she asked.

"All right."

"Come Friday evening for dinner."

A tiny white-haired woman, porcelain, voice like a much-used opera recording, a perfect articulation marred with small scratchings of age, waved when I looked around the train perform at Gravel's Point.

"Are you Joe Madison?"

"Yes, ma'am."

"I'm Fran's Grandmother. She's out on an errand just now."

The woman's dress faded and she wore glasses and she drove a Ford like millions of other women, yet could it only be imagination that her features glinted a special grace, her intonations extra elegance, her simple dress complete assurance, that in front of me an aristocrat sat with an old woman's life-loving smile? Could Fran's chatter about five generations of wealth fabled as Rockefeller's four generations have so influenced mind that I hallucinated a grande dame from a friendly handshake by an old woman in a used Ford?

Threw my bag in the rear seat and climbed in beside her. I, like Jefferson or Lincoln, a natural aristocrat and need fear no one. Customs must always bend to nature in the long run. But glad that Harvard taught me to wear a tweed sport coat. Everything deep loves a mask. What deep in myself? To do some great deed, to astonish the world?

The woman enquired how I liked New York, where I lived, and pointed out certain sights along the road. I remembered that everyone certainly Hemingway had laughed at Fitzgerald for saying the very rich are different from us, and I took a deep breath, laughed and relaxed.

The woman observed and smiled. I smiled back. Old age must always envy youth, and women admire men, so basking in that thought, I relaxed back on a sunny sand bank of the winding Washita and her smile became admiring.

Startling, though, first view of The Castle. That's what I called it. They called it home, but to me The Castle. Stoned and double-storied, with a mile of walkways, gardens, a forest, a house for a servant family, a half-mile sand and bouldered beach, a couple small summer cottages—

Mrs. Marble introduced "Mr. Marble." The gentleman, tall and lean, surveyed me professionally. Always have a ready role, and I beamed the look that made astute professors accolade "bright and promising." The old gentleman, hawk-nosed, slumped his long wool-enshrouded shoulders, pushed glasses back up his nose, and thrust out a skintight long fingered hand.

"Fran will be back shortly. Let me show you your room."

The stairways broad, the corridors look to be cold and draughty in the winter, the furniture old, solid wood, dark, as if they'd soaked their share of ocean water from the winds. I imagine the bedcoverings as always slightly damp, and in the snug warm sheets on soft full mattresses, among long nights of silence, irrevocably ancient heads lost in leather-bound Dickens, *National Geographics,* or *New York Times.*

Fran's old Studebaker crunched gravel. She dashed in, white band around her head, her long hair falling straight back, bare legs, wearing the same shapeless brown dress of the week before that ended two inches below her knee though every other girl in town had by now changed to the shorter style, also practical low-heeled shoes, ringless fingers, flushed cheeks, and excited clear voice.

"Joe, Hi! You've already met my grandparents!"

"Yes," Mrs. Marble said. "Why don't you let Mr. Marble take Joe for a walk around while you and I set the table for dinner?"

☆

Fran never again took me to see her grandparents, but in a way there was no need. Kept many memories as if a whole manner of life had been rendered up to me.

Had even come in handy at work because Rufus Brown, President of Worldwide Development, lunched with Farley Marble in Washington the following week. Rufus called me over. "I met an old friend of mine who turned out to be a friend of yours."

"Oh?" Probably Farley Marble. They're all Establishment, such as it is in the USA.

"Farley Marble. He said you and he had quite a talk."

"Yes." We had, so why say more? But certainly no friend of Farley Marble's. Still, nice of the old gentleman to mention me. Glanced down at Rufus Brown's immaculately polished shoes. Every morning the building bootblack stopped by and Rufus, without missing a syllable of his slow precise "exploring" speech motioned the old bootblack in by slight inclination of head, and, turning sideways in his chair, extended first one foot and then the other. A pocketknife could probably scrape away a sixteenth inch of polish before reaching leather.

Rufus always made a perfect composition in his suit, tie, and shoes. His sandy hair had thinned, but at fifty-eight showed no grey. A blue tinge to his lips, a tallow forehead, and flushed cheeks, shaved to appear hairless, told his inner exposure turmoil and perturbation eating away his life's diminishing remainder.

I turned from Rufus, smiled broadly at proper secretary Hollie, and retired into office, closing door behind. From out thirty-first-story window looked down at small toy trees on Battery Park, Customs House with its copper roof green, red ferry swinging into main channel, Statue of Liberty, waves on the Hudson, and two stark towers that would make Verrazano Bridge and suburbanize Staten Island.

Life fast approaching a minor peak, I gloated. Rufus sending me to Iran to make a thorough study and recommendations on the management of the entire enterprise transforming a giant province, and Fran, I calculated, would be mine within the month. Maybe I should even marry her. Western populist and eastern patrician made an unbeatable American combination.

Old Farley Marble, it turned out, after he's proved he could hang onto and expand his pile, had taken up New Deal politics in 1933 and after World War II gone back to college at the age of fifty-one and made himself an expert on forest conservation. Since at one time worked both as lumberjack and ranger, soon fell to comparing notes. What I remembered most, however, was the story Farley Marble told of Franklin Roosevelt.

Fran, I noticed sadly, threw out a glance that said she must stay absorbed in listening to her grandmother tell intricate details on some new knicknacks from Peru. Since Fran had built her grandfather up as almost inhuman disciplinarian and scientific intellect, I wanted her to listen to this human side, and, too, perhaps admire that I could bring it out of Farley Marble. But wouldn't waste regrets. Casting mind firmly from Fran, I tried to land every detail of the big fish before me.

"I went to Hyde Park one time in the twenties to see Franklin. Another closer friend of his and I were called to his bedroom when he woke up. We talked vigorously of some matters that concerned the three of us, and then Franklin threw his covers back. His legs, you know, had no flesh on them, bones and shriveled skin, absolutely no power of movement. Without steel braces, he could never have stood, much less moved.

"Well, he reached up, caught hold of a rung from the ceiling and proceeded to wing himself like a monkey into the bathroom, then he motioned us to join him while he proceeded through every detail of his toilet, some of it occasioning the most extraordinary effort.

"Don't you see, he was already thinking of returning to public life, and he chose this means of inuring himself against humiliation that might occur by any unexpected revelation of his weakness. My friend later told me that Franklin often had him present during this hour of the day so that constant exposure of his handicap in its most pitiable form would finally render its possession totally devoid of shame."

Edges of my eyes burned. Lower head a moment. Escape those old, bright, curious eyes still alight with power of their story, the bony shoulders slumping once again, the long skin-tight fingers slipping back from their kneehold to a position on the thigh.

Curious that I cried. So good to believe in greatness, in will conquering disaster. Relief. Relax. Deep breath. Caesar was great and Roosevelt not just a cunning politician and I, Joe

Madison, had a chance even in 1962.

Shortly after, when the grandparents retired, I and Fran strolled out on the lawn behind the Castle.

"Not here, " she whispered. "The moon's so bright you can make out colors of the flowers. Let's go behind the garden."

Like great blind eyes the row of light windowed bedrooms stared dark out toward the lawn. Would the Marbles actually watch? Intriguing.

Moon soaked through damp milk mist. Our fingers like polished sticks. Too boring. Must advance. Lips yield, thighs part, thin dress and panties, slacks and shorts all that keeps us apart, plus my belt's opaque wall with locked metal door. Sink to ground, flower odors, tough wet blades of grass, dull shoes, finger under the light bra bottom, what endless complexities, lips pushed apart, tongues between teeth, what the next strategic point?, move knee, who knows what she'll do, is it really worth it, here, tongues, moisture, teeth click, her thighs, knees turn outward, hand sliding into destination, moan, moan, shake your head feebly, why resist this, what'll you do now, should take you, pause, fumble at belt, grab her hand, shove it inside, shit, shoving bad, why no love, why not love, tongue mad along gums, drum gums, finger into ear, she's ready, now pull off—

"No, no, I can't—" eyes wide with moon, unseeing as moon, breakfast table, vase of flowers, mother talking to her of love and marriage, should I argue with her, oh hell, ignore, work her through, I never rapist, slow slackening of tongue, slow limping, slow stop of writhe rub as love death spreads through, why can't it die quick. Slow removal of leg between legs, now obscene without passion, yet pretend nothing's happend. Slow sit-up buckling door of belt wall, mosquito whines in moon milk mist, such silence, such ear ringing, what is it all for, she wants, I want, no, I refuse to beg. I'll never be turned down, formally I won't take, withdraw, let her advance if she wants so much, I can always do without, apart, her skirt's down over her sturdy knees, past the fine-haired thighs, she hunches forward, skirt pulled down over just-shaved fresh calves to top of ankle-bones, showed I hate, why aren't we barefoot, running, sadness, foreign, unbearable, why she inflicting sadness, should I have kept on?

"Let's go back," my words startled me, brief, staccato, final. Strength, determination, stone blocks Inca-smooth and indestructibly joined. Not even hold hands on way back. I'm strong and she shall not prevail. Why all so complicated?

8

At least three or four nights a week I pulled on blue jeans and khaki shirt, boots or tennis shoes and walked two blocks and across Houston Street's wide concrete mass to the Kiwi Bar. Houston Street infuriated me. Wide as major river, a hundred buildings demolished, gaping between Little Italy and the Village like Southwestern canyon, the lights set so that the little traffic on it stopped, started, stopped, started, sometimes one lone car on it took three minutes to go eight blocks of six-lane swath, mad destruction, who'd gained what?

Sometimes anger frothed out of me, I wished it solid like vomit to strew on Houston Street's ghastly gash, O quick, head for the Kiwi and a short twenty-five-cent beer.

Uomo universale. Men should do everything. And Toulouse-Lautrec could make a Moulin Rouge out of the Kiwi. Observe. Observe.

Walk down six wooden steps onto the wooden floor, the fish-net and rope dusty in the window, caricatures of all the first regulars on an upper beam, a few gone, like missing teeth, stolen home by those who liked too well and maybe also wisely?, paintings on all the walls, starting table-high at the small wooden booths, amazing no one ever seemed to scratch, write on, throw beer or whisky at, clean with spit or varnish with nail polish, though no holds hardly barred by Bennie, the owner with advertised heart of gold who tried to live the part, and the kitchen which never seemed to have a regular cook but always some new Kiwi regular, broke, pregnant, or confused, who made enough apparently for barbill and rent, and out the back door past the two johns into the terrace fenced by buildings on all sides with old awning covering one side and a slab of sky the other, and a cardboard church so identified by a chalked cross through whose carved-out door occasionally crawled in and out the bars mascot boy of six who's observed the Kiwi almost since birth and from this tapestried peripatetic schooling always answered firmy when asked what he wanted to be when grown-up, "Rich," and made the gray-haired bartender look sentimental jackass dandling him on his knee saying, "No, you want to be a great individual." "I wanna be rich!" But nonetheless crawled in sometimes for hours to his cardboard womb of church.

Yes, observe. But I loved Jeanine, woolly-headed, slim-ankled, knee bulging wide, deep thighs, deeper ass, narrow, narrow waist, grin, tight tight pants, lover of juke box, swiller of beer, of scotch when she had a man who bought it; occasionally she moved her head side to side like a Balinese dancer.

Difficulty. I always took eight hours' sleep and she always closed down the bar. So for a week didn't make it, though much exchange, once she danced oriental arms and head swaying on her stool in time to Armstrong, until hit the idea of going home, sleeping from twelve to three and back to finish the last hour with her. First time, that didn't work, she'd gone off to another bar with another guy. The second time, though, somehow we walked out together and down the silent Sullivan Street, the Irish ghosts long fled, even all the Franciscans looked Italian, but artists, teachers, advertisers, and Joe Madison, I couldn't bear to class myself, replacing Italians fast as they died because young Italians wanted suburbs that already were passe with Anglos they emulated.

And after she rich stream splashing into toilet came out, I reached for with nothing crippling desire though she too murmured, No, No, and her high breasts floated off as foam from straightforward body, lovely pleasure, she strong enough to take my strength unheld back by psychological tenderness, and in the morning, leaving, pulled back the sheet to imprint her body and could gaze without shock or any discomfort apparently only because she purple instead of red at the crucial point which, overcome, I reached and petted.

Sweating, three days later, decided to take her with me to a party of financial friends. Checked in advance. "Look, Lee, I'm bringing a Negro girl who's pretty great. Is anyone coming who's going to make a production out of it?"

Almost I saw ugly struggling with respect in Lee's eyes, but only a flash, and, hell, paranoia is prejudice. "No. Of course not."

Met Jeanine at eight. Horrified, I froze within, and could barely speak. She wore black slippers, tight blue jeans, and a white shirt whose tail she'd tied above her luscious naval open to the world on her flat belly.

Complicated. Couldn't tell her to go dress differently, couldn't take her the way she was. We began walking toward the party, she chattering, gay, I welcoming because could forget the problem and did forget it her problem, too. Halfway there, "I got to pee," she said and eyes darting desperately for concealment, scurried between two cars, let down her pants, squatted, and passed the yellow chemical down the gutter.

Pressed the buzzer. Worse than imagined. Western ideas still tripped me up. To my sport coat standard, Jeanine off the wall, but Lee, who'd said "informal," stood in suit and tie and spiffy shirt and, God, gowns swayed in the interior, and I heard Jeanine's voice dull. I flipped. I fell out. Panicked. What the hell to do, for this surely hell. Turn tail and run? Never Madison, Joe, from Western Indiana State, bullshit artist extraordinaire man who could milk minerals from moutain tits, but bravado puffed, pricked by glitter of Lee's stickpin alone, what in this hell of punch and gowns and tied and anal rigid asses, no time to check tautologies, whom I hated to the drear bottom of their bottomless nights of hard rocks breaking rocks to buy rocks for Miss Gotrocks, what to do?

To see with their eyes which I hated but which now my eyes their eyes her naval-exposing white shirt, dirty around the neck, oh, shit!, how could she be so unknowing about dress, why hadn't I said something so she could have changed or even made some quick excuse about not going?

Why had I brought her to this party of all parties? I never went to parties like this. Had I deep down wanted to cause a crises scene, to flaunt Joe Madison's independence to bastards despised for their endless talk of money, money, money?

Watched Jeanine submissively sit down behind the bowl of punch. Several people tried to talk with her. She replied almost dumbly, stricken smile. Everyone being so goddam good. If she white and dressed that way, they'd cut me and her both dead.

"Goodbye," she cried out. I couldn't mòve to stop her. Relief at her going, now would be dissociated from her, disbelief at my actually staying behind, amazement how rapidly she rose, a dream figure independent of conscious control yet compelling my attention, and slipped out the door, Lee holding it open for her, trying to say something, and finally settling on silence.

Shortly afterward, after assuring Lee everything all right, what a lying idiot I must seem, left and found myself running toward the Kiwi. Sure enough, Jeanine perched on a bar stool, in front of a beer, laughing and joking. Advanced eagerly towards her. Wham, she hit me on the shoulder with her fist. she laughed.

"Lousy, wasn't it?" Hope she didn't think me lousy, too.

"Those are your kind of people, Joe—"

Those are your kind of people, Joe, those are your kind of people "No, No, No!" I put them down, I had nothing to do with their money-grubbing and dress and address consciousness.

"Those are your kind of people, Joe," "No, no!" and the image of her, woolly-headed, dirty collar on her white shirt tied above the navel, whamming me and then continuing to laugh and joke with the latest guys she'd not known ten minutes before, cutting me dead, I who loved her—

9

The real problem, I often thought, ele-ali-excremental. The real romanticism abstracting the American soul to deathless because never alive into one-way-glass-looking-out sheen and glitter involves shit. The number of Americans who turned down foreign girl, boy, or whore fearing disease tiny fractional compared to number one or two day colon tightened with stored-up feces because no place to go but public or footstands slabbed in front of smelly hole (better aim good, buddy), or tiny newspaper-wiping European corners of hotels.

Ah, the American standards of shitting, highest in the world on its mind-lined dream throne, arm and back rest, good book to read, soundproof, soundless, being suntanned by ultraviolet lamp, with noiseless air conditioner set at desired temperature, humidity, stream of perfumed air adjusting odor to exact disappearance (smell a lower evolutionary part of brain, anyway, see ninth-grade biology text), and of course solid, brown, soft, filled with liquids (fruit, milk, and water) to proper consistency turd itself, regular, every day at most comfortable time, proper cereal, vitamins added, to give just the delicious touch of help, and paper so soft that one's fingers can tickle-stroke the itch most delicately, yet strong as steel so fingers never break through to dirty dirty.

The runs and the tights, diarrhea and constipation oh ye

classic scholars, are the true enemies of this world happiness. — Forgive the Romans for they plumbed the depths of plumbing and likewise we Americans, nor forget the dying saved from maggot swarming typhoid by this finickiness should the other, the tough and hardy Western image sneer and ridicule this sissy fop astride his sultan's throne.

The main thing, I hated about a girl friend in my apartment for more than a day was that inevitable could not be forever postponed. And especially when really loving, couldn't shake her out for an interval, had to face even the facts of underdeveloped America, close the one-half-inch-thick door, that didn't close tight, anyway, and through which every gaseous bark, whine, explosion, burble, murmur, machine-gun, rifle crack, sibilant arrow, everything but the huge soft really obscene gaseous billow could be heard, and so sweat popping out on forehead trying to artfully squeeze out noisless joint, except no matter the clever, the brilliant, the forever incommunicable kinetic triumphs of sphincter control, splash the traitor water gave away the shitty facts of clean-cut genitally potent logical understanding refined emotional Joe Madison, and sometimes a rapid splah-splash betrayed even a degenerate tendency toward the runs, that something unclean stalked the membraneous linings, disease, bad dirt, breath of death, stench of decay, and God, at times, once or twice only, thank God, splash-splash-splash of water acid-burning excrement waterfalling into the pure chlorinated healthy tasty toilet-bowl water, shamefully befouling the American sewage system that really was too good for anything but the best and finest textured shit, a man should appreciate and respect the finer things in life, certainly prostrate with shame at his excrement unworthy even of an Arab's shit-hole much less the Taj Mahal of New York's triumphal swirling fertilizer for its skyscraper trees, and then, then, final ignominy of flushing, the pounding anxious listening, will it stop, will it stop, the quick deft finger manipulation to turn off the gushing so as not to offend her delicate ears not missing a sound of all this bedlam madly screeching out that I was shit, the relieved buckling of the trouser belt – washing the sweat from my face, taking a deep breath, wondering whether it really worth it after all, and nothing in life quite good as cracked-up to be, but what the hell maybe I could survive not fucking but defecation—no, crapping! – no! Western image cut spurs into tender weakness—allright, all right *shitting*! One has to do it or die.

America, I thought, will not have arrived until perfected the pill that 100per cent converts eating to energy. But then the sphincter would atrophy, the lower colon, the upper colons, dryness, withering, and waste would creep toward life-sucking stomach unless swelled, petted, massaged, and flushed by shit.

(On Western pastures grass tallest on top of cow dung and when I boy crouched wind blowing sweetly between my legs, smelling strong and weedy smells, smiled to think I enriching, making more grass and pungent odors to arabesque the summer sky.)

10

The real problem, I often thought, not sex, not shit, not economics, but how to talk with people—people, hell! How to talk with anyone, and especially after you get close enough to talk about what truly matters.

The last weekend before departing for Iran for a month and I and Fran deadlocked. We kissed violently, softly, lingeringly, repeatedly, and our hands by now explored the entire coastlines and even up some accessible rivers of our bodies but the jungles deserts mountains prairies within unexplored.

Tremors, gusts, vibrations pulsated from within one or the other or both hurtling us into closer writhings but felt interpretation remote from the source and why of earthquakes as seismograph recording squiggles—I, thirty-two—experienced, "knew" of course that she wanted to end her virginity but that very abstract and not at all satisfying. She philosophized about life, youth, death, education, marriage, children, asked questions about the great glibly mastered Isms, existential, Marx, empiric, capital, and irritated answered letting-cursing self for weakness-irritability show, feeling that each revelation of impatience defeated me with Fran—should show only calm wise brilliance—but I didn't want to play professor.

What did I want? She'd come to my apartment the weekend before and lain with me on bed, naked, also she except for panties which my hand freely invaded and she responded but when I plucked timid as boy on elastic top like a question mark she quietly, "No, no" and my hand dropped like a whipped dog's tail and slunk from between her legs to the safer almost neutral firm skin of her belly which, focused on, separated from her and stroking it desperately, it almost reality of her enough, and a slight moan from her into my ears, and every half hour or so wondering what we doing there and then absorbed again in bits and pieces of her and her hand on me and her losing consciousness until timidly plunking the elastic top of her panties the soft, "No, no" wilted me again only to blossom once more in flesh sun and so on monotonous, tense, compulsive, unthinking, up and down, moist and skin, eyes of both closed most of time, unseeing, yes, truly unseeing, fingertips, hands, skin, spongy responsive underskin flesh, hair, moist, and night standing over us almost as if at once from the afternoon sun, night staring at us, and shivering, withdrawing, heads down, "Guess we'd better go out and eat—" "All right"—new kisses, half-hearted new attempt, then somehow refreshed dressing wonderfully quickly, relieved, glad to forget the threshing floundering hours, both bursting out to eat.

And she over lasagna and wine, eyes far away, skin alight, "we gathered around the piano at grandfather's place and we sang—why do you hate families so? Did you never have the experience of truly loving?"

And bitter, hard inside at my frustration, or frustrations, but she now concentrated frustration, I refused to believe in this girl's dream of her past, sneering inside that either she lied to me, to herself, or had been so skillfully lied to by her parents and relatives that she believed only unreality—but if she believed so, then could it not be reality?

I delivered hard sayings gemlike as I could carve on honesty, on old remembered Schopenhauer about Will and the destruction of the individual in his illusions so as to preserve the greedy species, Nietzsche on the genealogy of morals, and statistics on abortion, overpopulation, and general misery.

"Do you think your parents really wanted you? They did it

the night before and right after and even on that one night the on out of a billion that made half of you chanced to strike."

What were we saying to each other? Was she asking me to marry her and I saying no?

"You're so different from me," she said.

Feeling superiority in her statement, I flared, denied, yet often, feeling superiority myself, lectured and lectured about "the West where we didn't go effete like the East—"

She questioned closely, wanted to learn what I really knew about ideas, I grew angry, impatient. "Come next weekend, we really ought to go to bed together, you know that—" An appeal to her intelligence, her rationalism, her sophistication—

"I'll tell you something," she whispered, "but you must promise never to use it against me. Sometimes I want you to take me so much I can't stand the pain, but I will never be able to say yes, I will never be able to say yes."

Pride surged. She mine then if I would take—but I wanted more, yes, now I knew what I wanted, I wanted her to reach for me, I, Joe Madison, not about to plead with, truckle to, or rape this girl and demonstrate such need—

And why did she intrigue me so? So self-confident in her walk, laugh, simple even ugly dress, clean long hair, clean sweet skin, scrubbed and well-fed and doctored and warmed and petted since birth, never hungry, never wondering where her next job coming from, brilliant student, good singer, money as natural to her as air to others, good driver, capable in looking at maps, getting places, master of the paraphernalia of operating in American time-place dynamisms, conversant with Dostoyevsky and Freud as fruits rather than tortures of civilization, hot-blooded and promising of every sexual delight, nothing with her could ever be "nasty" or unthinkable but only absolutely pleasant, but I, I by God as good as her and never never would I stoop, my pride a match for such as hers any day, and you have to play the game of love by its rules of power or you're lost that's why all's fair, and so I always alert ready to end it any time she wanted.

Standing on Tenth Street and Seventh Avenue, "Fran, why don't we act like humans. We want each other, let's go to my apartment—"

"I don't know," she whispered.

"You want to just like me."

"Yes."

"Then why not?"

"I—maybe I want more—I don't know—"

"You want to just like me don't you?"

"Yes."

"Then, look, let's go. We can't just do all this over and over it's obscene."

"Give me a few minutes. I want to go sit in a church for a while."

"Oh! Sit in a church? You don't believe?"

"Just to think."

"All right. Twenty minutes?"

"Yes."

Striding around I came back, waiting for her, certain somehow of Yes, quite a good gesture that thinking it over in church, pretty cool, I bounded toward her when she appeared.

"Let's go. Fran!" I caught her arm.

"No." she said.

"No!"

"That's all I could decide."

Furious, I almost slugged her.

"Look, when I get back from Iran, will you know?"

"I'll try. Maybe we do need a break to think it over."

Why did it go on, go on, go on? I really ought to marry Jeanine, search out Lucy, become ascetic, do anything, masturbate, turn to boys,

"I love you," I said.

"I love you," she said.

I kissed her, crushed her ribs under me, convulsed against her, my body flicking like a whip and my semen poured over her and bed.

I pressed my head on the bone between her small breasts. She stroked my head. "Let's go eat," finally my head raised and smiled, magnanimous, victory from defeat, into her eyes smiling, and the two of us so fragile and tough seemed to agree accept fragility, too.

11

Scientific, tall, rawboned Bill Layton, drove me out to Eero Saarinen's TWA building at Idlewild airport to catch jet to Iran. This the way the world should be. Bill's left arm casually on rolled-down window, speeding out uncluttered (since non-traffic-jam hours) expressway, cities of millions flattened to a thirty-minute drive by concentrated technology and will, rivers automated into bridges, skyscrapers waving goodbye like palm trees, the random idiocies of the marketplace cohering like anything of nature's into patterns—city core, industrial ring, suburbs, exurbs, villas, spaces—machines mastered, used for purpose, I, small sack of flesh, in fourteen hours from Manhattan to be deposited halfway around the world in the land that once defeated Rome, ruled Babylon and Egypt and now posed still fascination, romantic decreptitude, cynical battleground and hopeful possibilities.

Taking off after Bill and I made our rum and Coke play at opulence surveying architectural magnificence of concrete technology bent into lines and shapes—superb toy to show off space mastery—I found death apprehensions. Always read of airline accidents. Bombs exploding. Pins falling out of tail assemblies and planes heeling too hard flipping over and out into drink below. Try to imagine one hundred people dying all together all at once. Including me. Impossible. Screaming, struggling impotent. Must be way out. Stay cool, probably most panic. Why don't they turn seats around, more safety. Why don't—and where's emergency door. Could I open if plane sinking under ocean?

At last surging into air. The plane survives the hard swing around that some pilots had publicly warned against because jet wings don't have good aerodynamic surface for it (whatever that means it means DANGER—to me). I relax and fantasy again power and fame in Iran and the glory of riding expenses-paid modern transportation.

12 Woke up this morning in Marrakesh a year and a half after that flight to Iran. I am alone. I don't speak Arabic. January, chilly at night. No job. Money's dwindling. Clothes stolen and I don't have a change. I don't feel I can ever work for an organization again. Can't ignore the several grey hars on the left side of my head, the graining of once-smooth forehead's skin.

Dream. Oh yes, the dream. We fighting others in vast theatre. Three of us from top loftiest balcony watching one of us chased into prop room at side of main stage. One of others follows and in dim light of that side room kills the one of us. He stoops to gloat. From behind a black weapon descends killing him and the door closes. Darkness. Someone is hunting both us and others! The door to top loftiest balcony opens—Enemies!—we pick up chairs, Something, not human, not animal, not even wind comes at us—to kill—

Woke up. Somebody coming into my room. Just outside. An Arab. I get up barricade door with chair besides locking. Heart pounding.

So simple. I hadn't told you—writing *Hamlet* without Hamlet. Writing you a good hip novel, melody line dropped, blowing themes that swing, but never that "I" writing this always-secret dream to be a writer. I figured do an interesting prestige thing—*write*—and reveal to you some surfaces of life we share. Fun. Work. Love. All good things. Save something from the wreck.

I know now why. I write to keep out madness not to make money or fame.

I don't want terror shivering hallucinating solitude so this paper and you imaginary reader now always with me my shield and salvation. Don't want to have to organize and scheme power again for monthly pay or capital gains. So since don't sing or paint well enough I also wish I could write for pay. I want big check so I can live, stay warm, eat good, buy books, music, throw parties for my friends, travel, talk to people like Stan today about life's meanings both of us astraddle fallen palm in garden of Koutoubia, mild afternoon wind swaying palms, cedars, orange trees, olive trees, the red nine hundred year wall of empire crumbling naturally away.

Imaginary reader, I write for you and me both because I need my sanity and daydream of your money and time to pass somehow and I still pulse activity.

Iran, Paris, Madrid, New York, Boston, Colorado, New York, Paris, Madrid, Colorado again, Grand Canyon, San Francisco, Tangier, Marakesh –that Iran trip caused it all. Or was it the people? Or my failure with Lucy? Or Bill Layton? Or Rufus? Or Jeanine? Or Fran? Or myself? Or with my mother and father? Or the world's failure with me? Or because upon my dreams, my yearnings, failure the verdict of nature? When shall I escape emotional causality, in mind I know endless vectors compose, causality only selective succession of events, why do I cling to it, to keep guilt?

Yesterday I arrived at Marakesh. I know that. I walked around the great red ramparts, through the endless intertwinings of the Medina streets, through palm gardens of ancient irrigation, gazed upon High Atlas snow, imagined Sahara and Black Africa on the other side, ate hot cheap soup from wooden spoon, chewed dry dates and gulped down oranges, a half at a time.

I understood Rimbaud.

I understood Hitler.

I understood Allah.

I understood that the walls of Marakesh and Avila were FEAR and that dogs barking on a rich man's property were FEAR. I understood that POWER and FEAR raised up nations and empires and wars and places and destroyed souls and were the eternally present apocalypse famine and scourge and could not be escaped.

I don't understand anything. I incant words but the magic formulas burnt and lost, I invoke forces dispersed and unknown. Religion and science conquered the world but mind disturbed turns on only magic and toothless hag incants mumbles invokes pity for a franc.

Let me be logical before I lose your imaginary money, imaginary reader, imaginary link to world. Innerly swagger I posed on my tourist-class seat prideful of transforming role to play in Iran, jet chargered knight into the Eastern night, and proconsul-like approval the flow of Americans on/off yet at London, Frankfurt, Munich, Istanbul, Beirut, Teheran, and thought of all empires of ever ours the best, most prosperous, peaceful (faithful *New York Times* and sometimes *Pravda* and *Peking Review* reader knowing full well the cost in blood and yet still say most peaceful) and well-liked.

A pity, I thought, all this so, our beggarly conscience bids us deny deny deny while everyone can see and many do in fact applaud. We should enjoy where so we slave.

In any event, at last Iran. Munster took me under his wing. German, forty, a legend, he labored in a hundred villages buying fertilizer. "You and I, Madison, I find we have more in common than some of my American friends. We can see these Iranians are children and that we must order and they obey to accomplish anything."

Thrills goosepimpled. At last reality. Hard hot geopolitical talk. Haushofer, McMahon, Hamilton, Nelson, and Drake. The real scoop. How things really done in this world and away from libertine liberal gossip that never dared beyond locutions circumnavigating hell.

Into jeep. Thin desert air and thousand stars like home, the Southwest. Faint stale smell. "The piss and shit of four thousand years," Munster laughed.

Neons. Boomtown. Taxis careering around statues to the Liberator. Oil even! Back home in Indian State! Adobe, movies, and there there the thud thud of diesel pumps hoisting water from the river and palm trees and women black shadows in head-to-toe dress.

The Bar at the Compound. I've been here. I've been here before. Movies, imagination, and books, these Englishmen on these stools talk as I knew they must. "They dragged the lieutenant, fine young chap, by his heels through Cairo before cutting him up."

And, yes, "Americans, you know, Madison, just don't understand the Iranian mind."

How did Rufus Brown get trapped in patterns? Why was it weird rerun and patchwork of history? German from defeat, Dutch from Indonesia's wreck, Italians on the make, French sad an witty at their decline and the new *èminence Amèricain,* and servant jokes, and justified fears of dysentery, and how the Iranians always answered Yes but what they meant if anything underneath those smiles who could say but only wait in hope disaster did not ensue.

And sure enough the cocktail party, the boredom, the rank, the intrigue, the long talks because no one knew my power with Rufus, none, or small, or much (me neither and less so each instant), the pressuring outpour "It's a great plan, Joe, it's really great, but my God do you know what happened with those bulldozers–?" "Do you know what happened in that concrete pour?" "Do you know what that bastard Sack did then?" "Do you know–" "do you know–"

A week later finally from the Compound and Administration with Munster to the field. In the distance over green fields orchards behind adobe walls. An occasional man or woman on burro paddling down the dusty road. All flat except far to the

West blue cutout of mountains.

We stop by a wall and dismount, Munster, I, and his three boys. He barks, they smile, and proceed to assemble certain small pieces of equipment. "Well, Madison," he says grimly, "you are about to see what this great scheme really does."

We advance past wall into orchard of gnarled and misshapen fruit trees, badly pruned, a jungle, sickly spheres hanging here and there. At one corner of the compound huts appear. One woman squatting washing slowly as if with immense effort a few pieces of clothing. Two blackhaired water buffalo drowse in the same ditch. A child pisses by the woman's side and runs from our approach.

I follow Munster between two huts. Four women loll wrinkled and uninterested against the wall, an infant crawls in front. Pieces of dung stacked on the rooftops to dry. Munster steps in front of a woman who's lighting four small twigs underneath a sooty pot. Tea. He barks at her and she looks up, humbling. One of Munster's boys put down a small rusty scale on the ground in front of her hut. Another takes iron weights out of his pocket and holds them ready in his hand. A third takes out a pencil and pad of paper. A dozen or more kids crowd around us.

The women disappears into the hut and emerges with three limp onions. One boy takes them from her and places them on one side of the scale. The second carefully matches the weight of the onions with his metal pieces. The third makes marks on his paper.

"I am measuring their diet, do you understand me, Madison?" Munster almost screams at me, "everybody tells me how much the people benefit. Nobody knows what the people do or eat. Only me. Because I measure. That is what this family will eat today. Three onions, weight ninety-five grams, now, see that piece of bread, three hundred and forty-two grams, now that rice, two hundred and six grams—let me tell you, Madison, you Americans have been here seven years, I came here fifteen years ago, not one Iranian with real education has ever come to the villages, they are ashamed of the villages, they go to Paris, to New York, to Hamburg, they are swine, they talk against the Shah, they say how liberal am I, I tell you they are rotten, they should hang from the trees, those liberal Iranians suck their money from these people their fathers own, and these people eat no better than before, they eat less well, because the army, the mullahs, the landlords, they all take more and that is what your American productivity does–I want you to see this, Madison. How many times has Rufus Brown been in one of these villages, once, I tell you, one time only. And that's one time more than any Iranian ruler. Nobody can stand it. Only I, old mad Munster, I go in to the villages, out of the fields, out of the big successes, day after day, to measure what actually these people get, and you see, Madison, now you see. Those women, they don't move, because they're old and used up Madison, they're thrity years old and they're dying of endemic syphilis, amoebic dysentery, malnutrition, and schistosomiasis–that's when they piss blood, Madison–all at once and they never see a doctor from birth to death and think it's all the Will of Allah!"

We drove for three days, village to village to village. Munster beat me into the huts. I watched chickens roost on babies in their cradles. "Animals! Animals they are and animals Iran will keep them but you Americans shout progress, progress, progress. Look and say we put neons in the city but what about these?"

Munster at times relaxed, donned a broad brim straw hat, and enjoyed bossing and adoration of his boys. He was producing a grand statistical work that correlated economic development, ditribution of new products, and social discontent. "I use village death rates," he explained genially, "these people are at margin of life. Any extra hardship immediately adds to death rate."

In spite of all, Munster believed. He wanted to build ten times faster. If he could have ruled, Iran would be transformed.

Back in New York, I told Rufus, "Munster is a genius. He should have more power. You ought to back him all the way."

Rufus looked out the window, skyscraper high with prestige

and success. "Yes, but perhaps he lacks balance."

In Iran for first time I understood about my balance. Life's an oyster. Enjoying it then am I whelk, do I drill, suck, prey, kill?

Taxi up from headquarters to pull me back from Munster's villages into the Centre. I make driver finally understand I want us to see ruins of Tower of Babel. Bounce and rock over side trail. Shepherds curiously stare squatting on top of old village middens. Mountain ahead. Huge. Crumbling walls. Half-finished French archaeology excavation. No one from Iran to guard. Everyone takes away pieces for Oshkosh or Dusseldorf souvenir, the human erosion outdoing wind and rain. Locals mined for adobe. Still huge, Taxi driver, an Iranian, had never heard of. Watches me smile while I climb up up up. Finally, interested, he swings legs out of car and begins to follow. On top I look at engirdling walls, each side at least a mile, can see river to east and river to west. Thirty-five hundred years ago how much larger, nobler, more prosperous than anything today. I gesture this to driver. He shakes his head. No one in sight. No sound.

Everywhere ruins are larger than Iranian life. Old dams with centre washed out. Two thousand year old bridges still used, steel only in the center, old city mountain middens towering above a village poor dull without a handicraft.

Dezful retains an old bazaar. "This city surrendered every time a conqueror approached and it alone survived three thousand years."

Ate local tomatoes and onions. Back to headquarters with the running shits. The tender skin of my balls begins to itch and flake away. It spreads onto my inner thigh.

Try to jot notes. Panic beginning. Rufus wants report, recommendations, understanding. I understand Caesar, Alexander, Napoleon, why can't I understand a piddling irrigation project?

I am Joe Madison, tall, lean, muscled, knocked around, understanding guile, sharp at numbers game, deep at production politics, at home in history in world developments, born to rule —I fall back on technique. First time in my life panicked on intuition. Signals coming in confusion. Technique: saturate saturate with talk, understanding listening, try to pick up good ideas floating around, look at the numbers, observe indications or morale—technique? There's no technique. There's no answer. No answer?

I fell to Teheran windswept on plateau ramshackle with spreading empty walls spectacular buying up, four-lane highways to upper-class suburbs, huge airport, new hotels, fancy American houses built close to the army base that glowers on the city.

"Tell me, Knudsen," I begin immediately with our Economics Analyst, "am I nuts or what's going on down there?" His wife bitterlips laughs and friendly like a conspirator places nuts and apples before me.

Technique: touch a man's uncertainties, bore in to problem center before he has chance to think, Bonaparte breaking vase in front of Austrian envoys, "Knudsen, is it all a goddam failure? It can't be bad as they say can it?"

Knudsen's forty-five. Fifteen years younger than Rufus Brown he never made it big before New Deal ran out of gas. Dreamer of high politics he remained analyst, now big time cynic but *man who knows*. Studies my face radiating sincerity, trustworthiness, and plunges.

"Of course something will remain. From a hundred million dollars something will remain. And that's something new for Iran. What could have been, Joe, what could have been—?"

The refrain. Since I've been in Iran, sour-voiced men, what could have been. My mother, what could have been if my father'd had more gumption. Father, if my mother'd somehow not been so nagging. Myself if only when I'd cleaned the house for you mother when I was four you'd kissed me instead of screaming because I'd spilt water. If only Fran, we could have loved instead of fought--If only—

I am carried away on the even tone of Knudsen's detailing impeccably the loss of control over maintenance the high rate of personnel turnover. I don't understand anything. I should to myself.

"Look," I said, "Rufus was the best administrator Roosevelt ever had. The TVX project's the crown of the New Deal. How could this thing go to pot?"

"What do you want an administrator to do, Joe?"

Scales from eyes. Rufus, alone in that skyscraper, no army like Alexander, only a name from the TVX project, discarded too soon from public life at forty-seven because American politics dwindled to cold war and private greed how could he have turned down Iran opportunity, impossible thing, to "run" a project this magnitude from New York, no power but a "name", a prose style that could dream "a future," the motivation of the Shah to avoid revolution, a people hungry for every shekel, every chance, taking everything they could get, believing from Allah, all bits and pieces. Rufus had to hold fast to acres of fertilizer spread, miles of canals dug and relined, tons of increased production, he had to avoid these tongues wagging confusion.

"All that we can do, Joe," thus Rufus with his shined shoes and immaculate top government official suit tie impeccable and noncorruptible martyr to service Scottish Anglo-Saxon Puritan who did now like to relax with a really strong drink or observations on bureaucracy tolerant/wise or hopeless/giving up," all that we can do is help them produce a bigger pie, a higher production, and know that after they eat better it'll be divided up some other way."

"How do you know it'll be a better way? The landlords, the speculators—" Kutuzov alright in novels but what the hell this for real. Plump-handed, ringed, sleek, fat, the man gestured to horizon. "I don't understand your American science but I want you to build electric lines to out there. All my land. I'll put up a thousand houses." His rents had quadrupled in price since the project began.

Inside I screamed. Rufus, Knudsen, Munster, me, working to make rich Iranians richer, villagers at the margin registering mistakes with death feedbacks. Working ourselves for much less than Iranian sharpers made from our toil. Why, why, were we the remnant New Deal, the JefferJacksonian American slaving for the greasy secret police army and landlords of half the world?

I talked to Sidi Malik. Sidi Malik claimed to translate King Lear into Persian in off hours. "We wanted you Americans to come. We wanted your production, your good things of life. But we made a great mistake. Because America has everything, we thought each individual American must understand all this, and we made gods of you. But we find you Americans are about life more stupid than we except that each of you has some tiny speciality, how to engineer electric lines, or make numbers march in a book, or climb through the mountains to measure water. You are fools and we shall get rid of you as soon as the project's built." He looked at my teacup, empty, which every Iranian offers when you enter his office. He smiled. I smiled. No more to say, was there really? We shook hands and I retired into the corridor where Iranians stood humbly, waiting for a chance to speak with His Excellency.

13

Fran airmailed that she in Paris. Would study year in Germany but could I meet her in Paris first?

I could not return to New York and face Rufus. No idea what to say. IMAGE: stride in. Rufus, my God, send me to Iran, I'll run project for you, you need somebody on the spot, life, ideas, talent—

You're too young.

I'm thirty-two, almost same age you took over TVX from Roosevelt. Believe in youth. Only no women in Iran for westerners. Fly to Beirut once every six months. Sacrifice worth it? My chance. Greatness. But he'd say no, anyway. I know nothing to offer. I can talk, inspire.

Never before knew my mind so full of words, mists, nothing.

I can't go back. Cable Fran YES. Cable Rufus SICK.

Golden leaves along the blackened walls of the Seine. Catch Fran and swing her in the air. Strength, love triumphant. We clamber down hands and feet on iron ladder and walk along the river. Laughing. Forgotten Iran.

"I have a room for us back of the Pantheon, not far from Notre Dame." Laughing, running, swinging, sweating slightly carrying my suitcase. We make it to the hotel. At me her shining eyes when deliciously asks as old conspirator for key from bright-eyes thin-lipped French woman. Up the turning dark stairs. Close the flimsy door. Bolt it. Doubt creeps into a pause, then we embrace. God, I hold her tight. Fran and I, we can make it. If I don't understand, nobody does. Whatever I say to Rufus will be right as anyone else. I don't compete with God but only other mortals.

"Not right now, let's wait," bright-eyes, retreating, "it'll be better."

Acquiesce to humor her, how could it be better?

Finally, after my impatient accompanying to Notre Dame, irritated at the phony tower pimpling its back with a Louis Napoleon figure procession, buying of sweets, talking her studies in architecture, returned. Shuck off my clothes and slip under the blanket holding her hand and kissing while she slowly undoes her armor. "Should I leave on my stockings—aren't they supposed to be sexy?" But to herself really, not to me. I listen, wait, how I need her, a month with no woman, in love with this one for three months, despairing of sense in Iran, but at last here in crucial area success.

She writhes like a snake. Words and intellect gone, gaping wet, tonguing, fingering, my plan to bring her to orgasm first time smashed, rouses me, her thighs mad trembling, I can't wait, think, plan, pound away black good drive done! Guilty but she leaves no coolness in me. Can't slowly appreciate, mold, lead her, roused to pitch I have to let go, take, and thus don't really take.

Later chimes of Notre Dame and we in time to that they end but we both take off.

And on till four in morning and we stroll to Les Halles. "Like priests all dressed in white sacrificing" she describes the men carrying the slaughtered red carcasses and a couple pinch her solid butt.

So at last my rich beautiful intelligent virgin and chalk another up but what Fran and I do now? I looked at her, jaw hard iridescent will. Can I last two weeks with her? Or better back to Rufus? Something has to happen. Bill Layton might be ready to go on a mountain top again. Where's Lucy? Jeanine, after all, right for me. She could cook fuck dance sing and who needed more?

I fought for control. "Let's go to Florence," I said.

"No, I want to go to Florence for a whole month next spring and if we go there for only a week it'll spoil it for me."

Michelangelo. I had to commune with Michelangelo *Terribilita.* What kind of damn did he give, dam didn't he break?

"But I need to go. I may never be here again."

She laughed. "Oh yes, you'll be in Europe again."

"There's nowhere else worth going."

We fell silent. "What about Spain?"

Good! Phillip the Second. Lonely, proud victor whom fate slowly stripped of magnificence because like Napoleon unlike Alexander/Caeser death didn't first overtake. We agreed on Spain. Another week taken care of. No have to think about Rufus Iran Fran or anything but chalking off Spain. Necessary to any man's full completed intellectual/artistic/spiritual life.

We relaxed, laughed, loved again, she came in waves.

14

I strolled excited as a boy from Amsterdam's Indonesian cafe section past the redcurtained windows staring at the bold blonde whores, comparing features, gown. At one house could not restrain my curiosity and dashed up steps to peer in second-storey window. Two old ladies gawking at television. God bless the Dutch and freedom, I muttered and tears streamed from my surprised eyes and if I'd only stopped, figured out what made that exclamation—but as usual didn't.

Image: sky gigantic thundercloud uncaring unquestioning turbulent, hurling lightning, rain, hail, when and how conjunction of all forces known/unknown impel fury garbed in fury, and bliss/hell keep revolving like cyclone origin itself.

In fit of irrepressibility pressed left index finger on left nose channel and blew mightily mucous out the right, picked then at harder stuff in left channel, farted, scratched, coughed and began running.

Always worried when didn't break into run for too many days consecutive. But anyhow when Clyde Moran used to daintily pick his nose with all enjoyment of old snuffing eighteenth-century French aristocratic lady drove me mad and we all tormented the lean lanky uncoordinated bastard and glad he never made above second string basketball even his senior highschool year but what the hell I actually tore and snuffled into my nose like hog after good slop—sometimes so carried away even in front of people carried on.

Fran'd brought me up short while in Spain. She'd said again. "You sure don't look your age." I rehearsed tales of torment, loves lost and ambitions missed, "but somehow they didn't seem to mark me."

"Maybe then you never really let them?"

Simple question or beady-eyed malice, Eve serpent striking? Hot rose tight in my bowels. "Of course I felt them!" How could she question? Not only most thinking, perceptive, but also most feeling of creatures, I.

"You recuperate fast." Simple statement, admiration, or criticism?

Take as simple fact/admiration admired. "Yes." But don't hold her hand for another fifteen minutes.

Returning to Paris on the train a tremendous quarrel. Almost forgotten in euphoria of Holland for first time, leaves dropping golden flooring on canals that Chicago gangsters could certainly use, bread, honey, butter, bacon, ham, eggs, coffee breakfast this morning by Vermeer maid, and then surprise at Rembrandt, to my mind stodgy painter of aging faces and bourgeois self-sat, seeing an arm around Jewish wife gleaming a luscious yellow buttery creamy golden played-in spatula'd heavy extravagant thick soupy stroke and feeling under that pride in woman-holding arm, muscles showing off secretively flexing slightly on beloved breasts, trying to appear motionless to painter, but Rembrandt catching that passion pride secret seducing flex, spatula'd smeared and gloated on gold gold yellow and love/lust it shouted love/lust/joy/mine/us it shouted plus painted smile I see, too, and let everyone see, see, see, and overcome I plopped in front and couldn't move though later intellectually admired Night Watch composition and played geometer in working out.

Almost forgotten that gigantic silence, that punishment I tried to mete out, because hurt at her coldness, that twenty hours of silence on the train ride except for tensely enforced casual cool courtesies.

And began when for first time we really made it, running down the night mountain road from looming Escorial, I unzippered fly, and nozzled warm yellow ex-me into splashing tracings and Fran cried out jealous but apparently happy at our turning on, "Oh, I wish I could, I wish I could—" but she stopped and dropped her pants though I told her of one girl I knew once who legs wide apart waddled determinedly forward splashing the downward stream like great sensual cow.

We became lost and searched laughing hand-in-hand the road to the railway station while chickens crowed and clucked away in adobe huts and once a head-on donkey stared at us in the night and air-feel grew wet hitting small puddles from the morning's rain that didn't star glitter enough warning.

Fran suddenly stopped, "Let's don't go back. Let's spend the night here. We can't leave now."

Why didn't I say yes? That's when it started. No it started when my mother first didn't kiss when I cried, no when the first amoeba put out its cilia and something chopped off, no when the first proton zinged into the second and met the repulsion because and not in spite of same basic thing. When ever started, at that moment festered because mean, unworthy, unadmitted to myself and guilt-redoubled I flared, mimic of her that morning, "Before we go to Escorial, let's get tickets back to Paris."

"But we've two more days for Spain!" I'd protested. We'd, at least I'd, been enjoying so. Never out of states before Iran except Mexican-Canadian borders though all over states "there's everything in America for those who want to see unless you're one of those provincial European-loving Eastern upper-class decadents with no two feet of your own to stand on" so everything in Europe I saw I loved and pulled Fran with me assuming she too carried away and nights I have up talking and fucked her supple youth mercilessly till each time she turned on automatic and gave one or more for each she got and so we bedded it twelve hours/day and short of time I hustled her around the other twelve and never talked out in slow boring words because so certain she felt it all—what did she feel? often wonder now—

"I want to see Hendaye," her stubborn jaw set and old Farley himself couldn't have steeled it more, her china grandmother no trace.

Anger moved in, show the bitch she can't leave me without paying dear—never occurring we both might like Hendaye, Spain hot in my blood and my seeing primal need— "All right," I said, "I'll stay here two/three days more and meet you in Paris." What Spanish girls like? Seville might be a ball. Joe Madison never anywhere but home though home itself a prison.

"Okay," she said, "I know you love Spain. I won't deprive you of it." Of course you won't, don't act generous, I look out for myself.

Long slow walk to station to confirm our ticket and meander by the empty grandiloquent Palacio Real where boys kicked agiley a soccer ball, laughs and shouts scrawling on margins of our apartheid.

At the window she turns, "Please come with me. Don't stay." What is it in deer's eye, dog's eye, most of all in woman's eye that stops the heart and ends all drive to kill, to master?

Finally, "Okay." In turn I begrudging but try to smile then fine real smile for after all I really like the girl.

Now after that backdown she wanted to drop out tickets, probably no refund, cost thirty dollars, all for a romantic night because we're really with each other in the dark adobe ducking below Escorial.

"Let's spend the night here," she urged again swaying her hip into my side.

"Look," I sawed away, "you said we go back, I finally agreed, and now we go back. Our ticket's already confirmed." Harsh hard defiant. She knew useless, perhaps also her mood gone. In silence found the station and began that long silent hate back to Paris.

15

But really it happened at Hendaye. We dismounted to wait for French train bitter thoughts of snow death Spanish Republic refugees Hemingway but no good since imagined them from waiting crowd at railway station cafe so obviously not but only dull victims of beaurocratic poor time scheduling and Fran and I excited to walk in our first provincial French city—Flaubert Balzac Stendhal—actually caught hands and strode out among sturdy pastels searching for the ocean. Grey clouds and wind, rain almost surely coming. Walked to out skirts and still no ocean. I begin to chafe because time going, worrying about train, and thinking ocean maybe still a long way off.

"Let's go back."

"I want to see the ocean," Fran said. "Let's go on a bit."

"It'll rain pretty quick."

"What's getting wet?"

"We've only forty minutes left."

"Go on back if you want," she said.

"Okay."

She headed off with her long winging lope, small of her back and forth so effectively.

Fat rain globules spattering then sheeting down by time I made it back. Ensconced behind cafe au lait under awning I enjoyed mediating Fran soaked bedraggled. I would be tolerant wise witting forgiving. "Fran, my God, sit down and have a hot coffee, no you'd better change, you're so wet—a great ocean, though, I bet—" no, that a trifle nasty. Well wait for spontaneous. How could I lose? Luxuriously broke the sugar cubes in two and stirred to dissolution in the brown hot liquid.

About twenty minutes later a small bus pulled to stop in front of me and Fran, bright-eyed, jumped out and ran to the table, dry as a dog all day before a winter fire. "Hi," she said, "Coffee good? The waves were splendid and this little bus came along just when the rain started."

You lucky bitch, you goddam lucky stuck-up arrogant bitch. "Sit down and have a coffee."

I couldn't think. Fury. A man looks at us curiously. "Your train's about to leave." And that was one of the reasons I'd given for coming back early, that not much time to catch the train. We hustled over and I shouted for us to catch the train on the first track, absolutely certain I heard "premiere." We stood there for fifteen minutes and no one else came. "This is the right train," I repeated obstinately. "The man said first track."

"Well, I'm going to see," she ran off and my heart sank for her French excellent mine poor and besides something obviously wrong. Her dry hair swung freely. If only she'd been drenched I wouldn't be so wild.

She waved. "The second track. Come on! We have to hurry!"

I showed her. I absolutely showed her how could I but I did the narrow selfish insolent spoiled intellectual nincompoop.

Deliberately sat oppostie her rather than beside somewhat spoiling effect by "Both of us have the window view this way" and studying deliberately the landscape and making notations on Iran in my worksheets thus hours that could have been precious poured concrete death on the first shoots of something approaching love. She finally concentrated on reading. Occasionally we both glanced up hopeless and on my part at least willing contempt with my eyes which maybe I now hope she didn't catch.

Love! I've never known what that meant. Months later by letter as we dwindled away by mail I claimed to Fran that such anger could have been aroused only by love. "If that's love, I don't want it," she replied.

Fran had a thing about "delicate quiet vibrations growing deeper with time."

Delicate. I hated the delicate. Of course desert flowers small tiny precise not what I mean by delicate, they survive dust sand wind heat drought. I mean finicky, easily breakable, "precious", "darling". But I never thought Fran might also mean something like desert flowers, I pictured always her grandmother's china and the time Fran had to talk with her for two hours about Peruvian trinkets while her grandfather and I talked important things.

If I didn't know what love, I knew hate. Hate a good thing if you hated rightly. No namby-pamby, anger and rebellion averted total tyranny, who could love oppression.

What's wrong with Iran. People there took it on the chin. Acceptance. Fatalism. Astride their asses trotting down the road, their women working, ruins everywhere betokening failure and end of all striving same why should they? Because at least they'd live longer and be healthier. For what? To ride in a train hating the girl they ought to love?

Ought to. I do not recognize ought. It's imposition, external, abstract, and somebody's making something out of it but generally never the guy who does what he ought.

Well that sweet bitch would learn in Paris who she dealt with. We were finished. I'd be off to London or Amsterdam, even Copenhagen. Another week before I had to see Rufus and I could cover a lot of ground. Spain not the only happy hunting. If only she hadn't made me confirm our tickets for now. How beautiful an Escorial night or two.

At Bordeaux a blond chic very Parisienne girl entered our compartment and sat next to me, reading Gide's *l'Immoraliste.* We three smile tentatively but too complex so make no attempt to speak. But as train whack-whackety-whacks on impelled to know her. To hell with Fran. No situation too complex for old anthropologically subtle Joe Madison.

"Pardonnez-moi, mademoiselle, cet livre la est un que j'aime beaucoup."

She turns and looks interestedly at me. I try to beam knowledge of literature, life, women, train rides, into her eyes.

"Gide, uh, expressent, expressent, oui? le soleil, l'afrique sensuel, de contraste avec la vie puritaine—"

We carry on for a few sentences when suddenly she bursts into giggles and grows three years younger. Her hair's dyed and she's a brunette from New York (Brooklyn Far Rockaway at that) and on Fulbright in Paris. Fran joins the laughter and the three of us talk but I concentrate on blonde and cold shoulder Fran out much as safely can be done. Desirous to impress both, high with emotional energy, language flows out describing Spain, architecture, people, landscapes.

Finally in Paris, Fran grasps my hand as we take leave of blonde who slips me her name when I request. "Aren't we lucky she came along and broke the ice between us so we could talk again?"

Oh, naïve as well as arrogant, you'll learn I'm not so easily appeased after humiliations heaped high. I mutter "Yes."

Difficult to find a hotel that night on the Left Bank. Fran's tired of our really slumming it and we try several on the Rue d'Etudiants but I'm obsessed that can't spend above ten francs and be true Left Bankers and I'm anthropological purist.

"Let's go on back where we were."

"No, I want to try one more," she says. I groan, she looks at me, then dashes into a hotel to check. All right that's the way you want to play. I'll show you how to play. I proceed without her, turn a corner, and panting hard, find a hotel, take a room, march up red carpet, obviously damn it an American students' home, English everywhere assails my ears from rooms, one guy tries to shake my hand, shake him off, slam my suitcase down on bed and sit writhing in satisfaction.

After ten minutes or so can't stand the pain. Run out in

street. Where's Fran? She couldn't give up on me that soon. Fran! I rundown the street, looking up side streets, Nowhere. Slowly I return to the hotel and fall to sleep exhausted but wishing she at my side.

In the morning huge cup of cafe au lait and two croissants which I devour in six bites. Famished when finished. Call Fran. Call Fran. Finally figure she'll probably be with French family friend. She answers, "Joe!"

Really where it happened inside me and her. But how potent this pleasure, sprawling quarrel across a continent. Ride waves furthest possible away from stone cold smashing center.

"We need to be apart a while," I lecture, "I'm going to Amsterdam. How about meeting at Deux Magots at four p.m. in three days?"

She agrees, sees me to Gare du Nord, and there I even take out my small overnight and place the big suitcase in her hands. "That's too much for three days. Take care of it will you? Thanks."

We kiss, break apart, and excited I look forward to seeing Amsterdam unhampered by another.

And yet I swear I loved her. At least I swore I loved her. That girl I eagerly left behind holding my suitcase while I took three of our last seven days together for many months off in solitude wondering how swinging a seaport Amsterdam might really be, full of lust to know every particle of the world.

16

Ramadan now in Marrakesh. Jupiter at meridian Venus about 30° from the horizon, and the new moon just below. Last night horns blew and today all restaurants closed except in the quarter of the Jews and down the highway in the New Town where Christians swank.

The sun disappeared behind the solid stone of Koutoubia with an apricot flush leaving the cafe filled with men. Soap poured but we waited till the exact moment. Good and hot, everyone hungrily drinking from bowl or scooping out with wooden spoon, breaking the day's fast.

And in the afternoon I shambled among the palms and tried to work myself through to Now where I'm also receding from just as from Fran then and Rufus and Lucy then still future now past.

At any rate, arriving from Amsterdam I met Fran at Deux Magots. "Aren't we worth talking it through?" she asked.

"I believe in face-to-face working out of the tough problems," I poured out the Harvard cliché.

"That fight we had on the train, it horrifies me that we could do such a thing."

"Shows we have a real feeling for each other. To arrive at peaks, you have to descend valleys equally deep." Gallop steamroll bulldoze with metaphor, I'll never be caught, chug chug.

"I think you could be such a lover—if only you could talk things out—"

"All right. I'll tell you. Why didn't you want to stay in Spain? Goddam it, if you hadn't been in such a hurry, we could have had the night in Escorial—"

"You were pushing pushing pushing me. I had to show some independence. I was going without you, leave you in Spain a couple of days, I should have, but I wanted you with me, I couldn't leave you. . ."

Slowly we healed the surface of our deadly wound. Even laughed about my anger that she hadn't got soaked with rain at Hendaye. "I knew you were mad. I was lucky to catch that bus, but I wanted to strut my dryness in front of you."

We skipped and ran across the Seine, through the Tuileries and to the Jeux des Paumes. I liked Lautrec and she Renoir and then we came to Monet's scenes of cathedral fronts. I backed away, complained for lack of room, criticized his "lack of form", and left with a somewhat sour taste but we took a splurge dinner and climbed to our new hotel room.

Every part of her body sweet warm ardent. We loved and loved till fell asleep exhausted.

Woke with a start. A breathless silence desert hush dream no not a dream but peer into back of my pressed-shut eyelid the Monet whirled before me and I felt how carping critical my complaints. That he had seen such colors on sooty cathedral fronts, that he could have so loved sun and transience and his mind blossomed such array and I only gripe at "lack of form"—my fingers sensitized to feel each grain of flesh on Fran's thigh, tears rolled from my eyes contemplating images of Monet's color. "Fran, Fran—" I kissed her, held her tight against me, she pressed back, unutterable, gasped, finally asleep again.

In the morning she out then back with long fresh warm crusty bread and jar of honey and we ate down with apples.

When I left two days later, looking out the bus window at her standing solemn in the grey rain at the door of the Invalides, could hardly have foreseen we'd never love again.

"I want something you can never give me," she wrote,"the delicate vibration, ever-deepening, children, home, and yet I resent that this makes me sound like the distended pregnant goat we saw at Museum of Modern Art for I want all that we had, too—"

And concluded with a precise description of Chartres, its architecture and her reactions.

Super-esthetic idiot—one has to make choices and she'll learn that you can't have both. Let her suffer with her future weaklings.

And through winter and early spring her image weakened till finally she wrote "it's gone." "It's frightening, that something that meant so much is gone." But this "feeling that's been coming slowly is now certain."

Stung, I wrote her what cascaded into mind.

Fran, I'm sitting at my kitchen table in front of crackers, peanut butter, cereal, the black reposeful Angolan mask and a copper Isfahan tray from which not quite all the tinny gilt's been scrubbed—and your letter's at my elbow. Just returned from walking the Village streets—a fine sleet slowly descending. Two small beers at the Kiwi reading a 'radical' magazine (i.e. jazz demonstrates US Black's sense of nationalism)—the bartender tells me of the time he had only enough money to catch the Greyhound at 50th Street & go to San Francisco—nothing to eat for three days except two candy bars. "A long time ago," he says, red-faced and mustached, Latinly erect.

My first impulse receiving your letter was to fly to Europe Easter and spend two weeks with you. In fact, after walking for half an hour and then eating my favorite pancakes at the Hip Bagel I decided *to do it, and strode out radiant.*

I reread your letter and wonder why I decided that. You say, it's gone. I suppose so. I don't cry over your letter because it seems useless. I feel like I am walled away from those whom I want to cry out to and touch. At moments they let me, and then they revert to their "natural" habits.

To hear you say again that "I think later on at best I would be happy with the smaller more delicate vibrations there can be between people who love each other—" nearly tears me apart—laughter, anger, tears. You seem to think giving up what we had gives such a definite certainty obtaining such 'delicate vibrations' whatever they are—look around you!—as if this were a real alternative to us! Tears for the disillusions to come, anger that you don't even realize what you've had, laughter at myself and you because we perforce take all this poobah so seriously—that for words, mere words we crucify ourselves.

On and on I chugged away who'd immediately looked up Lucy as soon as I'd returned to the States and had it out with Rufus. Life's Here/Now and you have to extract every morsel nor let any abstraction weigh you down. I admired my strength, my bounce back, and slitted honey mad a bee amongst a field of flowers but knew no hive to carry back my loot and so now and again stung to show I not dismayed by that.

American where were you with the great projects to save my soul? Where was I, America, with the great projects to save your soul? Where indeed were/are we, America, and anyone else for that matter? I sang of myself yearned to lose myself.

17

Fitfully sleeping on jet returning to face Rufus. Standing on porch at Grandmother's farm crowed with men listening to speaker out by trimmed Tamarack. Summer. Shirtsleeves. Leave my place by a pillar move closer to speaker. A dagger flashes into back of man who took my place and he falls dead. Instantly know they wanted to kill me. Run to side of house and bald-headed man fleeing. Chase him around back of house and start up other side. A tall powerful young blackhaired man points a rifle at me and I begin to retreat. He follows me from inside the house which has suddenly lost its solid wall and become only a screen. I slink closer and closer to ground trying to escape barrel's line-of-fire. Finally my head on the ground but the rifle slowly lowers and I lower and points directly at me. With good natured smile I shrug rise and slowly advance. Take the barrel of rifle delicately in left hand when I reach it and thread my way humbly insinuating toward the powerful black haired young man grinning at me positioned in grandmother's kitchen. When reach the stock realize he sees through me and will kill me. Have to fight. Launch myself at his neck but my hands will barely go around. Struggle. Growing stronger, my hands larger, I force him from the kitchen into dining room. A young woman with long straight black hair lies sleeping on a couch. My hands very powerful now I choke and choke and choke. His neck smaller smaller more pliable finally becomes membraneous cellophane attached to a small cellophane sack where the head was and a large sack where the body was. A squiggle of blood still forces its way back and force through ridges in the cellophane something like those in a hog's belly lining. I smash the cellophane under my knee and iron it flat with my thumbs squeezing squeezing until the last blood squiggle froced out. The young woman, her legs remaining motionless begins to raise her head and torso from the waist up. She sees us and eyes widen. "Don't kill him entirely. He may be useful for something later." I stare at her, acquiesce, fold the cellophane into a long strip, tie it into a knot, and toss it to her. "Thank you." I turn and stride out.

Waking, I forget what I dreamed then it struggles back, rushes back, I labor to relive it. My God, mother, I always thought I hated you, you sarcastic, nagging, tortured soul—and I thought I loved and pitied father.

18

Arriving at Idlewild my brain hardly had time for usual worries about death crackup and how to get out—Saturday night. Had to spend all tomorrow readying report for Rufus. Flipped through my fifty pages of notes. Obviously won't do. Organize subject matter. Introduction—state the problem. Problem is to facilitate management efficiency of Iranian Central Plains Irrigation Project. Problem is Knudsen, Martin, Smith, Hanley all told me they're quitting in a month if they don't get immediate spread, better distribution of product, training of Iranians to assume self-direction, money flow for Worldwide Development? Problem why the villages upset me when I've reached equipoise about Bowery bums. See steady and see it whole onward upward death not the goal and march in triumph through Persepolis the rest is silence.

Betrayed! That's the problem. Rufus betrayed me. Came to work for him in dumb affection, actually thinking he dead or old retired but hero of Andrew Jackson Roosevelt American past from his book – *TVX—New Paths, New People.*

George Malone eccentric Harvardite who cussed place going to the dogs, cooking Indian curries in tweedy grandeur, "when I was there, we treated people right. None of us would speak to Thomas Wolfe because he was a slob. Did him good. Developed his soul. Now they let in people from every class, every race, and fall all over themselves worshipping their 'genius' and 'potential' —ruin the whole lot of 'em." Anyway George told me, "You're tired of running a mill out West, huh, my boy? Well, I'll introduce you to a man who knows New York. He'll fix you up."

And this man, who owed George something, fixed me up with three interviews, boredom on his face at the imposition, and I trotted back to George with inscribed book from his friend. Of these three, all promoters, one assaying independence, "I'm starting space architecture." Visions of immense moon colonies, excited, I leaned forward. But what he meant, "All architects know how to do today is rear a huge cube of space. The client takes it because this is modern architecture, the latest thing. But actually he has no idea what to do with all the space, so he has to improvise or call in someone to tell him now that his architect's left him the same cube that everybody else no matter how different their function's got." His eyes glittered and gleamed at the profitable joke. It turned out, though, he would be engaged for months interviewing the "right people" trying to land a contract. I never heard from him again. We'd met under the Biltmore clock, that favorite for assignations.

The next had a scheme for speculating in commodities and wanted me to go 50/50 on checking out cocoa, copper, and eggs which, he was convinced, could be the holy trinity to real specialists.

The third, older, slower-talking,weary, and observant, was putting together a deal to buy out a large machine shop and needed someone to spur old management to produce counter-cyclical products. But his talk tinged with philosophy, I broke out politics, and soon found he was ex-New Dealer now playing with technological toys he was convinced engineers overlooked such as ramps up outside of buildings instead of elevators inside. At any rate, he suddenly stopped and said, "Rufus Brown. You know of Rufus Brown? Yes? Well, he's doing something very exciting in Iran. That's the kind of thing you're really interested in. I also know some other men."

Before seeing Rufus, I stopped by to see one of the others, James Wallace, president of Rockybuddies Heirs Investments, Incorporated. Heirs had about three hundred million dollars out, and four grandsons of the Founder (Robber-Baron capitalist Boom-Hero Peasant-Importer Castle-and-Titian-Buyer) composed basically the Board.

A two inch thick run covered even the corridor of that 58th floor office. Wallace, draped in intensity, composed his hands for a precise exposition. "The theory's simple. Rockybuddies Heirs, Inc. believes in science. Science is the base of all new products. After a product's established, the profit rate per dollar invested falls off—though of course (smile end smile) total dollar profit may increase. Heirs, Incorporated, is interested in profit rate on each of our dollars. Therefore we search out new fields, fields that perhaps are not even thought of as practical for ten years, let's say geophysical instruments for exploration of deep ocean bottoms, special metals for space housing or moon colonies, certain advanced types of transistors, certain catalysts, high pressure high temperature furnaces, or a chain of banks in an area we predict much future growth. We realize only one out of ten will become a success so we invest in literally hundreds of these concerns. (Here he rattled off a few and I sunk back astonished at the octopus reach). We of course make no effort to dictate solution of scientific problems, and often insist only upon one director on their Board—for after all, each of our men just look after many companies—and he assists generally only on financial matters or to ask questions from a cost/return standpoint.

"Naturally, he also advises us when to sell. This occurs when, one, we think the company will go under or is not advancing fast enough, and, two, when the company first achieves success. As you are aware, stock generally reaches such a peak at this optimistic moment that it takes sometimes years for even a sound concern to regain this height."

Q.E.D. No, never work for industry again where profits

the only measure, only real measure of the management. But I liked dash and go of private enterprise when it made up its mind, thought government slow/formalistic/bogged down.

So Rufus had the perfect combination—private-public. Image; (hardly listening to him explain) He my age when Roosevelt's long hand reached down, now his long hand reaches mine, the TVX, I Iranian Central Plains irrigation project, he development of America, I development of world, who knows how far might go—

I developed to him a thesis, "Worldwide just the corporation I can believe in. Dedicated to certain far-reaching social goals but carrying them out in practical ways influenced by subtle ramifications of economics, psychology, history, with a crew of top notch individuals who have or want no place now in American poltics but who want to earn their daily bread by doing more than producing a competing make of car that even if advertising succeeds in shoving down the consumer's throat only means some other production line runs at less capacity and no actual social purpose achieved at all. Worldwide dedicated to doing that which otherwise wouldn't be done just the kind of thing I can devote myself to."

Rufus bent his head downward listening and I fantasied he saw among other things vindication for his actions since could still work up youth. I burned and wanted him to focus the flame.

No wonder the airplane dream. Look and look for the father killed, to find the true father, the Philip who leaves us army and goal and Aristotle and whom we fulfill beyond expectation, that catapult to send us over the world's walls, that burning bush to thrill our souls with truth. But they betray us one and all. My father, why did you forsake me, and from where these thorns—did I not try to do exactly what you told me? and you did never recognize but rebellion and contrariness because you, you didn't realise your own words' content when they erupted at me, "Be strong, Be independent, If anything's worth doing, it's worth doing right. I hate a fence sitter."

Haven't I hated my efforts for years because I'm a slophound and never ran a lathe so well as I thought you did though ran away from home and studied how and again ran one in the army and what a shock when mother said, "Your father doesn't treat a car very well," for you so authoritative couldn't be less than practically perfect when you came out for something, and every mistake or fumble I saw you make thereafter a betrayal, doublecross, dirty coward quitting the game whose rules he made himself, because I lashed myself to keep those rules, and looked for him who would not fail me, for somewhere great men rode Arabian horses against the sky conquering Africas in twenty years building architectures music and gardens that any Sinbad son could revel in.

Doggedly, I charged you again and again as you pushed my head into the ground, shoved my shoulders aside, flipped me over, trying to learn how a guard charged past another guard to make a tackle. Why didn't you teach me to be a halfback? To throw and run instead of "You throw like a sissy" and so I grimly hung on to learn to be a guard and block and tackle and all that afternoon you showed me trick after trick exposing the green fool I was and I held back all tears, my khaki knees green-stained and torn and never did I think humiliation would end but even though the humblest position left from all my destroyed ambition I swore I'd learn to play guard and block ways open for the golden halfbacks my true loved brothers and charge into tackle and destroy the black furies that were our enemies.

And now, Rufus, you, too betrayed me. Let me enumerate the ways. The months before you sent me to Iran sometimes you asked me to lunch with you and sundry others. What made me rebel at your $4 executive lunches I'm not sure, but I hated them and you knew I hated them. I'd look around at stolid stoat gloat of brokers/bankers and think "What are we doing here? Where's the New Deal?"

I know all of us, even myself, could afford $800–$1000 a year for noon lunches, but Puritanically shit-thrifty or whatever I always thought of swine at a trough, with slop going to the human beings outside Harlem Bowery and Iran while swine feasted bored with their swill. Finally, I slipped away and ate at Nedicks, old antique sandwich joints on the Battery, seaman's bars, and on the ferry, and I was hurt that you author of *New Paths, New People* would not accompany though how happy when for a while seven/eight of us found compromise place and old bar/restaurant with 1880 paintings darkened on the wall, but it did have tablecloths and silver, and waitress looked like a human being if old redhaired and scraggly, – and at least I thought we laughed a little more, but I now wonder if I ever saw another human being–does anyone?– at any rate I built a better scene in my own mind about our eating at Barney's place. *For Ladies and Gentlemen* as the old engraved plaque said proudly preserved at the entrance. But the jukebox on the other side of the thin partition sounded music through and this disturbed and Barney's was abandoned.

Your immaculate dress and shoes. Oh I could continue with these petty things – you were different from my imaginary regal father because you dealt with opinion and place in the world and strove to keep Worldwide alive. You should have thundered been a Jupiter and I'd have died with you when they consigned us to hell, and even in America is it impossible to envisage walking poor and ill-clothed the highways (North in summer, South in winter) your disciple begging bread–?–Yes, perhaps it is.

And you betrayed me most of all, yes, out with it, because I really feared you and I wanted to love you, you to love me. You were my boss, you paid me, you instructed, I obeyed. "Rewrite that stupid letter your secretary sent out–and remember Worldwide can't afford slips like that." Crashing, nose bloody, the ground reared again and again as I tried to break through but the huge crafty figure sun besmeared with power pushed me in the rooty dirt. I can never be a halfback, throw that touchdown pass, erupt into the clear, out there alone alone alone with black forms writhing after me, failing to catch, the loyal and faithful cheering me on—

No, I knew I could fake nothing by you. My brilliance wilted, everyone told me I was brilliant, Fran even while I killed and desecrated on the train, my college transcripts, army tests, my buddies, but I knew what you expected. You expected truth about the Project. You expected me to do it right. I failed. I listened 16/18 hours a day to the tortured voice, I looked, I searched, I read the papers, I got the shits and itch, but Rufus, I don't know, what can I say? I know the project backwards and forwards, I'm positive, I know it better in the field than anyone, yessir, I'm positively prepared to assert that. "Tell me what you know, then."

"We're failing, Rufus, we're failing."

That's what I want to say. *That's* what I must say. *That's* my judgement. "We're failing." Send me out there your beloved and tell them you're well-pleased and let my try. Send me with two good men, Bill Layton amongst them, send me with the youth, Rufus and we'll do such things as TVX dreamed of, because there's worlds to be done and I, Rufus, this is what I can do, but only if you believe and trust and give me power. I will do without women, I lust for their sweet bodies, but Jung and commonsense set me free to masturbate if need comes hard with no misery, and I can take the itch again and we can do such a job, Rufus, as Darius or Alexander himself would envy, I mean old Munster will measure six limp onions on his scale and maybe even a piece of meat, I mean the taxi drivers will learn the history of their country, Beni Melik will meet Americans not tired out by wanting thirty thousand a year to do what they'd do for ten thousand in the States boxed in a specialist's bag, but even many of confused them sweating their balls off will roll and go because Rufus I worked up from the fucking bottom and I've done every job from shovelling and lifting to the big planning and I can tell real from phoney, by God, when it comes to picking out a man's working and Rufus, I can inspire, something other than sex thrill in Fran whom I can't really love, damn it, I can rouse the souls of men, but Rufus you have to say the word. Say it, man, say it.

19

But time's hurricane hurls leaves nilly-willy till disintegration. Revolution broke out in Iran's streets, students killed, new prime minister, parliament imitation suspended, and Rufus had to dig in just to keep the project going extracting funds by threats and wile for already commitments.

This I learned Monday morning excitedly entering the office but sense or cowardice enough to cool off with Dr. Vandermeer first before barging into Rufus and give my try a trial run.

And I—would I have said anything no matter what? Already that morning I'd revised and perfected what I meant by 'failure'. "Obviously, Rufus, I don't mean but that canals aren't being built—"

"I know what you mean," Vandermeer said. 'What's the good of a huge imperial project if all the souls engaged in it are embittered; if there's no joy in the work, if there's no increase of vision." Vandermeer former head of Dutch Sugar Trust Research fleeing for his life from Indonesian revolutionist had pondered in his exile.

"Yes," I said, "It's a monster. Something all should be proud of, something like a temple rather than a bulldozer—"

Vandermeer's enormous blue eyes gazed emeritus-like behind thick spectacles. "They do not want to hear this. They do not want to hear of this. They want to read figures that show success."

"If I don't get something done, I'll quit," I said. But could I give up my salary for first time in my life really enough to do as I pleased outside of work hours—Who else to work for besides Worldwide? I stood on precipice, at the brink and no way down.

I wonder how I looked coming through Rufus' door. He beat me to the punch. "You're upset," he said in his precise way. "You have a lot to say about what you saw."

I looked at him briefly and saw really nothing only felt that he already had taken position I couldn't play halfback but green had fallen on my face if I stepped lively might make a first string guard now. "You should send somebody else over—awfully thin on management—my God, how they talked, everyone talked to me at least four hours, sometimes four in a day, I had to walk away from them to get any sleep at all—they're starved to know what you think, what role they're playing now, loaded with ideas to contribute—" Sounding like an idealistic sophomore, I imagined Rufus recoiling with faint disgust at my lack of control.

"Some men lose sight of the final goals," he said. "They have a place at one stage or another of the project but they cannot see it through as it changes from planning to engineering to management to training."

All I'd brought grist to the philosophy mill, no action, I could see that. Ten years of bending my back to army, to engineering, to administration gone, became only a dream of experience. I knew or felt I knew I was pegged "unreliable and emotional, may be occasional use for his mind—"

My fault. Why hadn't I prepared better? Where had I run out of gas? Stalled in a business desert, I would now spend years at sinecure as buzzer response to answer certain problems.

Rufus had seen many come and go. Weariness wariness steady in his blue eyes and red sinking cheeks bulldog holding on to what he knew, complete the canal system, complete the canal system and perhaps knew he'd die the day it done—first new canals in twelve hundred years in Iran, and after all who was he to judge as I so definitely did that men's spirits could be improved—the work, that was what he lived on, as TVX lived on, the spirit lost, but the work incorporated into the States, as the New Deal lived on, Rufus did not play down the value of work that would produce goods for men, how man divided it up, that was the business of the men of each present day but something had to be there before division could contend. Rufus had his shoulder to the wheel and wise wizened he asked not—except after four drinks at cocktail parties—whither and whence but did what he could do.

Finally I shrugged. "Of course, I'll write the whole thing out. You should know though that Knudsen and Hanley at least will quit if they don't get definite assurances of a change."

"You really think so? Perhaps. The cost is high." He sunk his chin on the two thumbs of his joined hands.

I left him knowing my world with him finished, and knowing, too, I had nothing left, no place to go, no more ambitions to try another company—I would hang on with Worldwide to see what happened. Like dying within. I could blithely play with Fran because knew higher things engrossed my mind, but now nothing holding me to heel, keelhauled I wandered like a rat that night from all my sinking ships and got drunk at the Kiwi, had an old time sake's beer with Jeanine, staggered home alone, and massaged to come remembering sentimentally Fran's response and made it by cutting off her head and taking her from the neck down only.

20

Bill Leyton buzzered my door and burst in dawn. "Know what I've got here, Joe?"

"What?" Rarely seen him so excited.

"Peyote."

Cricket hot afternoons in Indian State and a Cheyenne astride his horse clopping through the willows near the sandbar on which I almost snoozing watched a dragonfly trying to imagine him twenty feet wingtip to wingtip geologic ages past. The Cheyenne plashed his horse across the shallows, flicked his eyes at me once, bluejeaned black-hatted saddle-slouched disappeared into the blackjack remnant of lordly yore.

My anthropology prof years ago leaning over, "I joined the Wichita tribe last week. The peyote rite actually gives them god to eat. I didn't believe it, but now—perhaps—"

I never took anything druglike into my system. Horror of it. No smoke, oh yes of course alcohol on occasion but not much. Well, chocolate, tea, coffee, coke (Coca-Cola that is), lots of sugar—but for example no aspirin, no benzedrine, no sleeping pill, you think I'd ever let chemistry affect integral purity of my Joe Madison's Greek and lucid dome? Rather my skin crawled with lice. One time I had breathed pure oxygen, and of course under ether once, and dentist the two times gone shot me to painlessness, the Cambridge police fired their gas when gleeful we students crowded them, and of course carbon, carbon monoxide, carbon dioxide, rotten eggs, sulfur dioxide, all the sooty acrid city air, gasoline, methane, butane, oh god the time they poured milk magnesia down my throat when wormy kid and out white wriggling mass poured and Uncle Mike cut them up with a lawnmower my grandmother, mother, father, all laughing me too so glad to see the worms slice and sliced again by whirring blades, untold chlorine pounds drinking and swimming, anyway my precious system non-chemically defiled I often said except for water and good (good?) foods I'd never put to wrack and ruin of drugs of any kind.

Dumas fascinated me with hero's description of his visions, but mostly I thought only one totally beyond the law, avid for all experience, could so risk, one needed strength of Damascane steel to escape the snare, though wasn't I all that and actually I'd liberally lectured on occasion the stupidity of our drug laws, which all scientific reports showed worse affects if anything than from Prohibition even.

"Oh, Peyote?"

"Yeah. Sixteen of the little jewels." Opening a paper sack with surgically sure motion of his gifted hands, he pushed toward my face like oats to a horse.

I plucked one out and contemplated its pale blue-green, the tiny flower tuft in center and soft spikes.

"You ever had them before?"

"Yeah. Twice."

I sat down surprised. Bill and I like brothers for three and a half years. Really something if he hadn't told.

I'd arrived out at the Cooper Mine just south of Four Corners, supposed to run the grinding mill and flotation circuit, fairly nervous because of some reason dream of mine to run a production plant and wanted badly to make it hum.

For a hundred miles by road though not as the mythical crow flies to towns over a thousand in any direction—well, ninety-three miles one way lay Flagstaff. Mountain ranges exploded to the view in three directions when you climbed high enough out of the canyons to see, and they dropped almost sheerly down to deserts tiered in levels cliff flats so that from subarctic to subtropic flora fauna nearly always within two hours drive or less from each other—

Image: At last on frontier as my grandfathers and eleven generations before them—comforts and boredom stifling everywhere but this one last place. I'm really 'out there' and Joe Madison helps bring epic to a close ring around the rosy and the rose dies but fun making the ring anyway, dust bronc flash of sweaty haunch and ride 'em, guy, ride 'em. My cousin Shin at fifteen rode Brahms in the rodeo kissed the girls and made 'em cry poured in twenty points a basketball game (school too small for football eleven with all its logistics of another eleven minimum for reserves) and dead at sixteen from truck smash-up whom I adored wiry tough and we clod fought, charged with corn spears shrill cries, and punted the football higher than grandmother's dusty elm trees leisurely back and forth passing time under the blue sky (generally) and on the musty stiff brown grass waiting for the Christmas dinner putting an edge on our appetities before eating into that lovely torpor probably much like starved pygmies from the elephant they've trapped.

Also occasionally cussing myself out for coming to such a lonely spot (made special trip to New York before leaving Pittsburgh steel mill not only to see Glenda—first artist I'd ever made it with—but also to stock up on books fatefully impulse buying among the others Nerval, Rimbaud, Baudelaire) and wondered to whom I'd talk freewheeling about whatever popped into my head.

Thursday after our smooth-hided personnel man with sleek half-inch uniform padding of fat to keep him warm doubtless since so cold inside pale blue staring Alabama eyes with soft drawl incredibly from hard mouth showed me to the once-green but now mostly brown dusty here and there agglutinated into balls from specks of grease staff house with laughable because really not so reassuring boulder from the back cliff reposing by its side, I sat down on my cot and slowly unpacked my things. Personnel had said, "Youah the first man in youah pohsition to stay heah at the staff house in a long time." Stares pale blue why don't they at least water you bastard. "Most men in youah pohsition are married." Get lost, Jack.

When finally propelled myself to investigate the staff house quite reassured. An Austrian-born bull-shouldered mining engineer with thick boots, meaty ham clapping my back, and hospitable whisky bottle, philosopher of management foibles, a lean, almost spectral other Indian Stater, khaki beclad shirts and pants, with lore of side roads, side trails, and lonely spots where still a man might fantasy himself the first, a Jim Bridger of undiscovered (to English-speaking white at least an always thrill—) regions size of football fields—too bad no bigger but even tiny Americas he felt hard to come by nowadays, and three other men of tolerable aspect.

But best of all khaki showed me a room now vacant but occupant of which would soon return from Yucatan the very name tingled me wide awake. Khaki opened the door to give me glimpse and I danced, actually I believed hopped up and down in sheer delight.

Navajo rugs adorned the floor and cot. Katcina dolls from every Pueblo or so it seemed gazed from the walls befeathered, painted, carved with vigor, pots with abstract design, with deer, with birds, of flaring shape, stashed under the cot, the desk, on a special shelf, from a corner, a mask gravely grand glowered, *books*, a shelf of books on Indians, the West, and chemistry, two rifles, and all arranged with such effect museums should emulate.

Well, that's how I met Bill Layton, from his rooms and I could hardly wait until he returned from Yucatan.

"You bastard. Why didn't you tell me about peyote before?"

"Hold your horses. I brought the goodies over didn't I—no use talking till you're ready—isn't that a Joe Madison saying?"

I leaned back, "Shoot."

"Wa-al," Bill and I the corny but we loved it joke of really stretching out a Western drawl when we came to something intimate, "Louise got me on it last spring before I came here, and when I went back out while you were in Iran we tried it again."

"You could take longer telling about it."

"Joe, I saw pink, a pink number-six snooker ball."

I waited. "Yeah? I've seen a few myself."

"That's just it. I saw a—one—pink, real pink, number-six snooker ball. The prettiest thing I've ever seen in my life. I couldn't take my eyes off it. Finally I cried it was so beautiful —I can't look at pink now without wanting to stop, soak it in."

Bill and I had a habit of closing down the Company Commissary most nights at Coppertown. We sat in one of the back booths leaning against the wall, one leg stretched over the seat and sticking out past the cage, the other under the table, talking or doodling away, on and off animated would swing our legs under the table and face the other, or when a buddy came by would wave them over and chew up whatever he had to contribute.

One time he told me, "I don't think I have any feelings inside me."

"Sure you do. Everybody does."

"I'm serious. People say they feel joy, sadness, worry—I don't. I just flow on and on."

"You're bound to, down deep enough."

"Well, I never got that deep." He communed with himself.

Always polite, ready to discuss any point to whatever time needed, expert driver, always ready to explore territory new to us, hiker, gifted chemist—and yet I knew dreamer of wife, home security/love backing up his labor in the world--perhaps it was possible.

Carrying on this way about crying and the color pink—must have been extraordianry.

"And the second time?"

"Wa-al," he laughed, "not much happened but I don't think we took enough."

Long silence.

"You know quite a bit about it?"

"About Lophophora Williamsii, you bet, Mescalin plus a few others."

"What does that mean?"

He leaned toward me. "You should have seen Lou. Truly extraordinary, the way she reacted."

"How, how?"

"You can't explain to someone who's never had it." Silence. What the hell, Bill's going to take it again and I better see what he's doing with himself. Aztec wandering far out in the desert, lost, tries everything possibly edible, hungry, thirsty, chews a bit of sour plant, suddenly new energy, visions, makes it back and five hundred years ago incorporated into way of life no Amerindian wasn't I sick of all go/go/go what better time to try?

"Where's a good place to take it?"

"It's got to be a good surroundings," he said eagerly.

"Well, we're not out West."

"Don't you have a couple girl friends at Virtue College? Why don't we got up there?"

"Maybe they would. I'll try–"

We shook hands firmly as though we'd never met, true brothers because freely adopted that we had been. To hell with authority/father and girl/mother a brother/comrade was only where trust could fully lie. From the wreckage of the world fraternity equal alone could save the free.

21

History shattered. Hardpan of shallowplowed and overfarmed, once buffalo-grassed and bluestemmed, drilled through overturned and steaming vapor to spring again dig down fingers for good smells and tiny hairy interlacings that once again can watersuck through droughtiest heat till grain's borne aloft and grandfather placed me in the bin of the old combine and down cascaded smooth cool golden polished grains upon my head of hair bare shoulders back over bluejeans, some slipping down inside the belt, and on my feet and through toes and laugh thrust hands upward into burnished stream close eyes let beat on upraised face and down the curving slide of neck and chest burying me to waist supple write in almost water-fantastic gold.

I sat alone from Bill and the two girls Indian-legged in the center of Virtue College's hockey field, great green grass sward how fit for true dance orgy drums trumpets girls and guys unhappily never to be consummated, falling grass blades individually bent underneath my weight contemplating jet bomber B-57 black above the sun not far from setting.

Let him drop the bomb, I'll worry no more about annihilation of all meaning, the Edamite tower a crude mountain of adobe ruin to New York's sleeker babels, but thirty-five hundred years of rust would leave little steel, metal loves to return to earth. History exoskeleton vising emotion down to insect size circles spirals vortices or whatever geometric corset seems to fit whereby generations reduced to slavish labor for pyramid, skyscraper, rigor mortis till war re-convulsion Hitler Attila Tamurlane destroys, terror, then slamming on all brakes see forbidden's necessary you must not touch you must not touch your god, your neighbour, neighbor's wife, father, girl, boy, mother, and if even you look and slight touch desire ripples pluck out that eye and the other too if necessary don't play with fire it burns eternally, don't, don't, don't, to keep down Hunnish Blackman terrors, the killers from the mountains outside and gutter slums within, storm trooper clerkish hearts gathering Germanic tribes on world's subways and traffic jams because vast that's evil departs like cloud but little that's good coheres to orb sub urbis eternitas and e pluribus they'll make ONE allright snack bars in Paris and Buddhist armies in Viet Nam because universal world vision Alexander, one brotherhood Iknahton, numbers Pythagoras, zero from India, algebra from Arabs, Calculus take your pick Liebniz Newton who cares now, Grotius world law, Constitutionalism Anglo-Saxon centuries,keep your secret police O Allies we understand freedom takes time to develop sure does narcotics squad FBI income tax CIA obscenity censors time to gain true freedom and individual respect YES SIR! hop to it, that's individual respect and pity primitives—what would happen if called them primals?—because they dance sing loaf fuck and ceremonial war kills one or two a year magic souls and shiver our spines because no plumbing when digging up old Indian camp noted grass still grew higher where old best fertilizer landed and all culminates America Common Market Red Square Egyptian radio and Peking pomp work work work fight fight don't don't don't touch and your death pushes humanity onward upward because at least it's lebensraum n'est-ce pas tovarishch, huh?

Like a huge hard turd it fell rocklike out striated and waterless history from catchwork days, which charming or horror story do *you* pick? but yet I also had speeched bespeeched ORGANISED my God spiritual piles and blood distended from blooping effort of curled striated agony but HISTORY did fall out and shattered.

Tears streamed down my face watching that jet black bomber move so slowly trailing Euclidean rainbow lines "You poor bastard, you'd actually drop it if they ordered, you'd actually drop it, and never know, you'd never know, you poor unlucky bastard—"

Bill and I had found the girls and we planned a perfect day. "Surroundings all important and the people—" he'd said. "This stuff's potent either way." Excited, adventurous we prepared.

Virtue College seemed ideal. Back of its giant more than hundred-year-old-trees and stone well-spaced buildings a small river ran into a dam and formed a lake that sparkly lights in its dark-green clear day color fell into white froth passing over its obstacle underneath a wooden red-painted bridge upon which girls alone, together, or with dates had stood and nearly always looked downstream at disappearance and mediated.

On this lake canoes. And we began in early afternoon to paddle upstream finally past the college towers at which the girls chanted laugh/resentfully their soul mother's (but in fact) soul shyster's) slogan Faith Prudence Truth they overcome we ironical escapading experimenters hooted and hollered, beached canoes a quarter mile down below a corn field under far-over-the-water-bending oak whose streamward elephant trunk goggled out but drank now only at floodtime, looked a moment at each other undetermined how to enter water oh inescapable questioning is it really and I doffed shirt/shoes/socks/wallet and plunged belly dive bluejeaned into chilly Indian summer current though sun out for past week and Bill/Nancy/Doris looking laughed and stripped down to shorts panties/bra "Don't look till we're in" they called and we merrily swam waterfought flirted and waved to an old farmer who peered at us from behind his fence row.

Coming out, we dried-off with shirts and blouses and truly friendly now the girls lay back to soak some light relaxed in their brief things and all but. We breathed deep and easy taking moment by moment our buildup for Bill had convinced us all scared that little cactus and though underneath, he and the girls later confessed they too, moved fear/wonder/hope at what might happen to our jiggled minds we played to hilt the game and opened-up our souls.

At four-thirty we returned canoes and hushed now searched out a place. In a grove of oaks a stone fireplace by gravel walk off the field hockey green expanse. We set our four bottles of pop--to be used as chasers, taste-killers--out by blanket side and while girls talked quietly a background of red winged blackbirds Bill and I cut carefully sixteen cacti to quarter-inch size dropping them in an aluminum pot, fluffed a *New York Times* book section and made a fire. The girls fell silent and we all watched the water turn black from the boiled pieces. Bill refilled the pot after it'd boiled down and again we watched. The flame burnt steadily, waxing waning only from combustion of the wood because it was a charmed windless day.

"It really tastes like shit," Bill said judiciously remembering.

Nancy ate some anti-throwup pills because she feared she'd be almighty sick. Doris started to borrow some, then didn't. I resolved to emulate Bill's actions.

"Don't know exactly how this liquor'll be," he said. "But I know it tastes so bad I'll never eat it again, maybe this way's better."

Finally it boiled to his satisfaction and neatly laying out four glasses from his for-years-full-of-peculiarly-appropriate-things kit, and placing a strainer over each in turn, he poured four quantities exactly, to the eye, level each with each. A small amount remained black among the boiled cactus sections. "We can drink that later if anyone wants to." He looked at me wryly.

I opened the four pop bottles and passed them out. Bill handed out the four glasses.

We all on our knees, the two girls on the blanket, Bill and I on the grass by its side and looked at each other and at our glasses of black fluid. Deliberately to enter unpredictability!

Finally Bill raised up his glass and we all quickly followed. Hot, bitter, revulsive the fluid worked down my constricting throat, I took a giant gulp of pop and estimated the huge remainder.

None of us spoke but concentrated on our task of finishing the glass, occasionally eyeing the others to compare progress. With an impatient motion, Bill finished off the last third of his glass and then drank down the remainder of his pop, vigorously swirling it in his mouth before swallowing.

I finally finished my last sip. The girls stopped with over half theirs gone.

We still sat on knees leaning forward, staring at each other, waiting.

"When does anything happen?" Impatient.

"Pretty soon, ' Bill said.

"How do we tell? "

"Probably first you'll begin to see all sorts of colors in the trees. "

"I see all sorts of colors now. I studied the impressionists." Irritated, it'd begun to seem a kind of hoax.

Doris lay down on her side. "I feel like I'm going to throw up."

Nancy sat backward on her haunches rotating her knees up under her chin.

After another five minutes I began to feel restless and quite independent. "I'm going for a walk," I said. Nobody answered. About thirty yards away I sat down on the gravel behind a bench.

A huge rusty spike had been driven through the two-by-eight, grey, ridged, and splintering with age, holding that part of the bench together. Someone had drilled out a circular hole for the head of the spike to rest flush against the outer surface, but time had loosened and it protruded an eighth of an inch or so from the wood, being slowly worked out doubtless by the pressure of countless resting backs, some slumped in rest, some erect with parent's visiting pride, some undulating from a kiss and feel. Rust lay thick as a Martian desert on the round spike head, red and grainy with here and there black specks of iron carried by the oxidizing rust from the metal surface slowly losing strength, atom after atom succumbing once again to lovely ardent oxygen, the spike bearing up under the shearing downward of the wood weight probably sometimes up to a hundred pounds when two fat arms hung dead weight on the bench back, would the spike give way first from backward working out or crack from downward shearing, almost an impulse to find a rock and drive the spike back in, remove the rut and polish exposed surface, but who was I to interfere with what was wondrously taking place. Long ago a workman looking at just this place drove in that spike, someone had thought people will like to sit on benches, designed a solid back on which one could lean for hours thought or idleness, carried it to this grove's edge, cut the grass and graveled this access walk, here thought, caring, skill conjoined with use, and I, privileged spectator, sat on my duff in the gravel undisturbed to see this pageant pagoda by.

"Bill, Doris, Nancy, Come see!" But they huddled uncaring on the blanket, the fire down to embers, their nearby oaks vibrant with thousand sheens of green flashing from shadow so dark it might be everlasting cave within.

Slower, I approached them. Doris giving small throwing up noises. Neither irritation nor sympathy. They have their world, their digestions, and I have mine. I shall not let them destroy this moment.

22 Dark and Bill driving us all downtown WOOLWORTH's lured red evil fascinating and back of neon the brick wall assumed red red reflection shadowy but seeming to indestructibly burn among the brick.

Invading eating joint, I ordered banana imperial, the rest whatever they desired. Nuts exploded hollowly in my mouth surrounded in creamy sweetness, but across a family filed in and we turned in horror to each other. Hate on that father's face, murder in the mother's, fear and future kill engraved on each the four children, silent they ringed a counter arc and woe to him who should loose their wrath. Uneasy I smiled to Bill and Doris/Nancy nodded our nod.

We fled cops spectering our mind and outside investigated eyes, found pupils large, and drove to outskirts joint where hamburgers made fine delight.

Driving back through town Bill stopped. "Look," he said, "I can see right through that Church wall. The Church of the Fourth Dimension." I tried to see, couldn't, but did imagine.

When I'd walked away the second time from the group of three and stood in the field's center, alone with grass and sky, Bill appeared by my shoulder.

"I'm glad you came."

"The girls are getting better."

"I really didn't care. Something was happening and I had to

follow it out."

We stood shoulder to shoulder and watched color begin to spread around the sun. Suddenly energetic I dug into the ground, then sat back observed the bomber and escaped that kind of history.

Doris sprawled out on the red bridge and Nancy joined Bill at the tree's edge. Jumping up, I dashed halfback twisting full sprint to Bill and Nancy whose summery dress ended halfway on her thigh and whom I wanted to romp with right then there but Bill's my buddy, she's his damn it, and I repressed except to whisper madly in her ear, "whatever happens, right now this moment I love you," and dropped to my stomach and began excavating from within a tree trunk hollow to ground level light piles of sawdust, glistening sap honey, and small black ants, so clean/good inside and why'd I ever thought damp dark rot—

"How come Doris's having no effects?"

Bill laughed. "Did you ever see her sitting sprawled out across a bridge before?"

After seeing his Church we parked out in the corner of an observatory yard, Doris and I made it on our walk from the other two, and we all lay down Bill Nancy me Doris side by side in Blankets/Navajo rugs Bill and I brought could see Bill/Nancy hadn't made it Bill's cigarette glowed red dark red as he puffed slowly stars so many stars above and a stream of sparks arced oh he must've flipped his cigarette and wildly then heart beating knew I still wanted Nancy so holding Doris one side my other hand crept fearfully to Nancy's side and what a back and forth of Bill's occasional hand, mine, and Nancy doing nothing maybe sleeping but I skating on desire's edge mad just for her touch—

Morning-sun-grey feeling-tired-finally left the girls and drove back into New York.

"Orange," I said.

"What?"

"Orange's my color."

He grinned. "Pink's still mine."

"I can never thank you enough," I said.

"I'm glad. I still felt nothing."

"Come on!" I almost disbelieved. How could he have failed to share, he who had introduced me?

Fourteen, John and I hiked back across the railroad track by Marge Hunter's high elm trees and over mulberries scattered red at alley entrance and up the grass centered rutty peaceful hedge-channeled alley where lurked only the Fredericks' barking spaniel when ping and ping again.

"My brother's shooting at us," I yelled and we dropped to our bellies. We laughed because couldn't believe it and probably he wasn't trying to really hit but we crawled on down one of the ruts.

"Hey, Rog," I shouted, "You playing a joke?"

Ping. His high-powered air rifle cut loose again. John and I lined up behind telephone post sideways covering us from Rog's angle. The BBs bounced off the other side.

"He's only trying to scare us," I laughed.

"Yeah." John said. "Some brother."

Out of ammunition finally we charged him and he fled into house and out the front door as we neared him.

"Aw, let it go," I said, shamed to the quick my brother did such a thing, why did he hate me so?

Genial Joe Madison, lean and smiling-faced, always had his buddies, his girl, big man who knew the score. Father who betrayed me, sarcastic mother, brother we mutually didn't speak, sister I had never had but lavished fond imaginary incest on—

What is mask and what is man that I am mindful of it anyway who cannot assure a cubicle to my name and all my thinking ends in eating, running, scratching, shitting, fucking or trying to, or good solid cud chewing idly moment passing those the greenest pastures perhaps—

"Bill, goddam it," I said, "you're more than a friend. You're my true brother."

He rolled his Ford down the West Side Drive and New York glittered electric high and promising us all ambition and to the right the Hudson rolled dark now down its ancient trough to that ever-saltier ocean where life once began but since the sea/ air changes also, life could not now repeat should anything annihilate.

23

I was finished then, but I didn't know it. Frog legs kick a long time brain severed. Grandmother brought hens Rhode Island Reds from the henhouse to edge of U-drive Granddad graveled around his high prarie house, deftly swung them around and around in air gripping their head and the body flew off sometimes thirty feet away yellow claw legs kicking wings beating and occasionally up and ran a foot or so blood spurting from severed jugular and Grandmother tossed the dulling but still bright-eyed head eyelid closing down, to Spot and Morning Star who sniffed toward the flopping bodies but knew better, though soon as Grandmother took inside for hot water and plucking, circled back to lick blood spots, and sort of purring snarl. Eddie, half-Sioux, and I in the San Juan cabin, cold day winter in the air spruce sweet and rustling like the sea when Eddie grabs his .22 and puts one right, almost exactly, between wildcat's eyes that we sat so silent had actually walked to cabin door and the cat stood stood stared fanged rippled writhed gradually rigidified it seemed ten minutes don't have any idea how long finally Eddie sitting for the whole time with rifle ready but awed by cat's response not pumped another gingerly approaching boot-high kicked it over one final thrash and that was it. "Everything wild hates to die," Eddie said who reminisced sometimes of Calamity Jane's last days when he a kid she daily fired revolver shots in the ceiling and laughed or so it seemed to him and to me hearing him curses or rich smokehoused memory.

WildJoe Madison with all regret masterwork of mask carving, fetish, Westerner booting it through the once Philadelphia banker-owned White House cussing stomping drinking white lightning, scourge of the money changers, Arabian horsemen non-Versailles betrayed by Normal Status Quo swooping on the Babylonian Whore, and reveling after melting down the cross of gold in gleaming cups, at the same time under that deerskin shirt a heart sensitive to the subtlest most-raveled-girl's yearning soul clouds that a city treadmill dunce however rich and university log-jammed with learned lumber could never hope to perceive with his artificial eye, while behind that drawl the Corsican, the Macedonian, the Georgian mind that came on Provincial but lightning calculator unhampered by queerish foibles outread outthought the intellectuals who amazed could only say Voila un homme what Goethe should have said, and besides all this likeable cuss who gets along with anyone.

That all dead but too many twelve fifteen twenty depending how you count it years not to go out convulsing.

Not till ten months from that November when in August camped in the Grand Canyon rim with Lucy and our friend Sally did the dying cease and that after rending with Lucy that deadful winter—there was much and tedious dying to be done and little life but that little intense enough to look at once again.

In interstices of mask, I felt gypped and life-starved, ignorant, lashed from post to pillar. My cousin Bo approached me with his .22 when I and cousin Liz exploring the ruins of Granddad's old bran mill, I ten and Granddad three years dead from his fight at sixty-eight with government man but the bran mill in ruins from years before suppose it served the first settlers out on the plains when they covered-wagon'd in from Texas, anyway Liz one year older than I and darkened long haired she'd let me sit in her bedroom and watch her comb. Bo motioned to remain sitting in the circular pit brick-and-mortar

-crumbled-brush-filled that reminded of the large storage cellar while waving me up for ma's talk conference which since he fifteen, cardriver, rifle shooter, singer of songs, flattered me no end.

"Joe, you want to shoot my rifle?"

"Sure," I said.

"All you have to do's one thing."

"What?" my interest died for Bo exacted real values.

"Come on, now, hardly anything at all."

"What?"

"Just say a word?"

"You sure?"

"You believe Bo, don't you, when he gives his word?"

"Yeah—sure."

"Just say a word to Liz down there."

"What word? I don't swear."

"I know you don't, Joe. Just say, Fuck you, Liz, loud as you can."

"That's all I have to do?"

"Sure."

"What's it mean?"

"Just means Fuck you, that's all."

"Come on, tell me."

"It's just a word they use around here, that's all."

"Can I shoot twice?"

"Joe, all you have to say's one word. One shot's enough."

"You're sure it's all right? Liz won't get mad?"

"Look, Joe, aren't we all cousins, you and Liz and me?"

"Yeah."

"Why'd I do a thing to make Liz mad at me?"

"How'll she know you had me say it?"

"For Christ's sake, Joe, do you want to shoot the rifle or not."

"Yeah."

"Well, I'm not going to stand here all day because you're scared to say a word to a girl."

"All right. All right. I'll say it."

"Go on then, but it's got to be loud."

"You sure it's all right?"

"Go on, say it twice and you get two shots."

"Two times?"

"Go on. What're you waiting for? Shout it twice."

"FUCK YOU, LIZ!"

A million miles away her small head turned. I couldn't stop.

"FUCK YOU, LIZ!"

None of us said anything more. She looked at me for a few moments longer, peculiar, distant, sad. She turned to gaze down at the pit bottom, all brush filled. Aunt Marty talked of rattlesnakes but I never saw any, and I felt brutal and senseless and lonely standing male triumphant at this word power with tall Bo grinning but it seemed uncertain and as if he no longer quite so strong.

"Give me the rifle, I want to shoot."

"Okay. Here it is."

I fired twice, rapidly, at a distant crow and missed. I walked with Bo on back to Grandmother's house leaving Liz alone. I was afraid to talk to her for three or four days and we never mentioned the incident.

I didn't know from nothing and I read a thousand books and did a hundred jobs and listened to countless stories and philosophies skulked the neons of a dozen cities waiting for a car to stop and take me to tapestried fulfillment and walked the trails of ten mountain ranges waiting to see a mountain lion jump a bull moose while a grizzly batted trout to her young.

Waiting. I never admitted waiting. I wouldn't wait. Man of action. I drove ahead, life is short, cram it full, you make your breaks in this life, master of fate/soul/and if had to would Ahab sink the ship ultimatum to Cubas actually thirteen years before I had intellectually punked "now's the time *before* the Russians have the bomb to take the world." Swaggerer who'd never then taken a woman only whores in Mexico and an older woman me.

So started calling Lucy that November. Very involved. Saw

her two or three times at excited, frenetic parties at her place. And in January it began that which most I shudder from.

24 Koutoubia strikes a loud drumbeat against the sky each time I look at the black cobras sway intelligently observing their handler now and then launching a strike the fat sluggish asp vees its head lowdown against its body little incipient feet crawling from cool concrete to warm blanket when put off and I and Arabs of djelabas army jacket boots slippers sandals shoes every rag of Christendom and craft of Araby crowd in circle the music of the handler's three assistants charming me if not the snakes and I breathe deep for I was drowning back then and air's so good so good when the lung's tortures cease.

This morning a figure—bull hooves and shins, two-legged, the bone yellow black hard digging into grass crushing the blades, above the shins flesh, a human knee, haunch, buttocks, penis, almost fully erect, firm bag of balls and from the top of pelvic girdle a Cobra swayed, huge hood a foot across, flicking its tongue, all this outlined against what customary perspectives would make call a sky composed of white writings dense hard flat above green level grass and in front of the figure a bamboo flute played by red lips and long fingers.

August I lay naked under sheet and blanket in the still living Old Frontier Hotel Streeter of Durango, Colorado, unable to decide what to do or what might happen Lucy and Sally preparing themselves in the bathroom down the hall would enter any minute oh if only we could spend the night loving in all combinations, I knew both separately from winter deemed both beautiful and since they headed California while I out on Western project met them to guide two days through canyons but all so well we'd just decided onward together to the coast and the two had sat one on each knee holding and kissing me on the balcony above oldtime piano and the two tired girls in netted hose and garters remnant of mining splendor serving the main street and oil men till it'd become clear to all of us I should leave my room and join them how we all knew each other by that time and how little.

I orgied in my mind with two houris but uncertainty because knew very well two complicated psyches bestrode colossi-like these worlds of flesh.

Sally came back first from the hall bath. "Hi," she said.

"Hi."

Turning her back on me she doffed her clothes, and smiling sweetly, climbed under the cover I flapped open for her. I kissed her and the lovely soft warmth moved full but not passionately against me don't foul it up Joe no moves too quick to enjoy the sip. Lucy entered.

"Already in bed, ha?" she removed her shoes, stockings, skirt and hopped briskly in. Kissed her briefly and we lay then all three backwise, I at least staring at the ceiling.

"Sally's sure warmer than you, " I finally said.

"Oh," moment's silence, "you mean Indian princess has stripped down." Sally giggled.

Lucy jumped out, removed blouse and bra but kept on her panties. Never so close to several of my fantasied ultimate delights and curiosities but we lay still, one of my hands on one each breast.

"I've decided never to sleep with anyone that I really love till after a long time," Lucy announced. "Of course if I'm only going to know someone two or three days and I like them then I will."

"That sounds grossly unfair," I tried to sound benignly sagely humorous but inside howled to myself you bitch it's absolutely unfair here we're sailing and last winter you know we made it good at least a few times, well then, well once at least for goddam no-ifs-buts-maybes-sure. Why the hell not me now since she fucked those short-term others. Of course worried about her goddam mental health, not healthy like me take anything, it'd be perfect tonight, it really would, you both know it, don't you, but Lucy's the resistant one I think. Placed a leg between Sally's and devoted both hands to warming Lucy.

"I want to build to something really good with a man I love," she continued in her pleasant but unpleasantly firm voice though she crooked her back against me as I cuddled those two not classic shaped and not large though large nippled but nonetheless unforgettable and I loved them saucy breasts.

"Loving helps build love," I pronounced after mulling several ways to say.

"It didn't us last winter."

I congealed and slowly the ice age crept from inner digestion out to hands and in the long silence I pretended they went slowly asleep and nerveless and then turned away as in a sleeping gesture but probably Lucy actually asleep all that acting wasted as often my best histrionics because we'd driven three hundred miles and hiked around two mountain passes that day and long emotional talk down to bar balcony below but stalking and lust nervous turned hands to Sally but she put her hand on mine one inch from the happy goal though content enough in stroking her anywhere else. How I hated liberated intellectual women no matter how soft, beautiful, what insights, souls, and whatever other paraphernalia they carry around inside. I wanted my fuck orgy, nothing crude and simply but real artistic with these two fine clean girls the perfect physical specimens together with esthetic capabilities but in the name of building healthy psychic structures or out of many fears or who knows what they wouldn't I didn't ask nor talk it out maybe menstrual or maybe tired as hell but I not calm enough to reason lay on my back fuming frustrate chained by living desirable flesh and finally rose gently snaking and untouching over Sally and tiptoed out to my room careful not to waken.

Still couldn't sleep. Alright, Lucy, you win. I might still love you. You I want not an orgy not imagination just plain ordinary right off making it even just to hold you and I'll give up dreams here a trois. I got up, and stole down the hall again, knocked softly on the door, no one stirred and slowly opened it. Lucy's long blonde hair lay on the pillow faint in the Main Street lamp light diffusing though the second storey windows, Sally's dark hair almost met it since they both slept rears in knees out and heads only slightly out. Nearly softened my heart to see such sleep and yet wild at feeling I'd been had that night, brought to stare in the window at rich people's feast but forbidden to touch. I had to move ahead. Action. I knelt in front of Lucy's sleeping face and kissed her cheek gently. She stirred and stretched her arm brown from Mexican sun across my shoulder. "Ymm-m-m," her lips chaffed slightly together.

"I kissed her again, more urgently.

Her eyes opened and stared. "Why aren't you in bed. What's wrong?" I felt like a fool. She'd expected me to stay. We three could have had such playful fun awakening in the morning. Five days to go on trip, anything might develop and such a sound trustful base then. I couldn't do it determination I'd backed down to Rufus goddam Joe Madison moves forward when he starts and takes the consequences come what may nothing's had for nothing each man in his prime or not pays many prices.

"Lucy. Lucy! Come lie with me in my room a while?"

"What's wrong?"

"Trust me, Lucy. I need you, I need to really hold you." I hated myself for using need. Hate need. I don't need anybody. Man born alone dies alone all real thinking soul desert journey's alone my mother in the kitchen finally, thin-lipped, "I don't care how long you stare at me like that it doesn't bother me," and I gleeful because had focussed hate hate hate on her and it had bothered and I was getting even for some monstrous thing she'd done to me only I know I'd never get even nothing I could do would ever make it even for I'd been helpless and she'd done some obscene cruel caustic thing and you never admit need because that's a weapon against you—

"All right," she said. "Go on back and I'll be down in two or three minutes. What room number?"

"Eleven."

I'd ruined it all again. Just like I had in January. Because I couldn't wait. Why was I so desperate?

Control. Joe Madison had control. Joe Madison stared winter blizzards down or at least into them till he brittled with cold. Joe Madison mastered his subject matter. Joe Madison tried to outwork, outthink, outfuck, but never really tried to outfight anyone who'd ever worked for him and guilty as hell about the omission in the catechism and could take it or leave it and amazed girls that he really could amazed himself anyway but now where control? I'd have to show her. I wasn't the whining beggar she thought to have been kneeling at her bedside. If she wanted to be cold I could take it just as well as her she'd better not make any false interpretations from a three o'clock in the morning moment of weakness. I didn't need Lucy Moreland, if she didn't want to least as much and even that was some stooping *more* than I did then to hell with it there's a million others like her and now I've learned how I can find 'em, Fran, for example, just as much on the ball, Fran gone, too. Women distracted men, every Western always ruined by some simpering heroine who understood nothing, man in proportion to depth oriental in taste for women poor old Nietszche under his sister's thumb, men should turn to simple uncomplicated girls, Jeanine laughed, slugged me hard on the shoulder, "They're your kind of people, Joe," "No! No!" Lucy entered stood by the bed.

"What's the matter?"

"Nothing," I said. "I just wanted to hold you. Too restless in the middle of you both to sleep."

"I'm sorry," she said. "But I can't do anything with you right now. I'm fighting to make it through to where I can do that and everything better. I can't risk an upset."

"I understand. Go to sleep." She back cuddled against me and I held her. I didn't understand. I didn't want to understand. Her, I wanted her right now but what afterwards might I want? I suppose I understood her but I hated my fucking understanding. If I were just an old deprived hard-up boy they'd probably let me do it but I'm Joe Madison and do understand and strong I don't need but damn it, Lucy, *underneath*. Underneath! But I'll not let you see. At least I'll never just out and say it to you, you'll have to guess it from my mad actions, and if you really loved really truly you would so that proves you don't but what the hell only a blithering lying optimist shallow brain too soft for life expects understanding.

25

In those beginning days also our culmination as far as joy we'd planned to drive down to Washington (Lucy had a car, spanking new Ford deluxe, one of first fruits of her Trust estate now fallen into her hands I hated cars as owning one myself though of course out West different from New York. There as Bill Layton always said it's your nomad steed but in the City they destroy. Pity Europe that bitches about Coca-Cola but produces cars cars cars their cities headed toward bulldozer their villages toward Main Street there must be a better way) to see a couple friends of mine, both married, curiously and unusually almost exceptionally appearing to be happy with their state, not doddering dull content but somehow vital.

Lucy, "I'd love to see people who're living not dying with each other."

We'd already had a rocky comedown from our first high and I plotted these four days off Friday through a Monday to take us out away and show new sides of versatile Joe Madison to Lucy who seemed to think me almost a racist Anglo-Saxon I putting down her ardent political carryings-on almost casually as screwed-up blonde blue eyes in hot revolt from stuffy wealth naturally turns to Negro jazz almost absolute necessary phase in early American Sixties I pontificated sociological we made it fantastically in bed when would this epiphenomenological bullshit cease and Lucy just relax and she and I really—really, what? I didn't want to marry her or even move in—what even dream we were moving toward? Another death convulsion?

"You make wonderful love," she said glowing-eyed hands back of her head, and I pride-glowed, "but always to me never with me." What in hell do you mean by that I didn't ask hurt and flabbergasted. "But that can come later," and she raised her head so gently to bring her lips to mine which turned cold but I pretended anyway, not understanding why she criticised at time so close/warm.

The first day, the third time I'd called to see here since back from Iran, and this time she free for a Saturday afternoon and dinner, almost unbelievable she so busy with people/events. And everything that moved seen through summer-calm, wispy clouds color, color, color, and took her to the Kiwi but she no eyes for local color leaned across the little table and soft rain her lips against my forehead cheeks lips chin. Somewhat embarrassed my eye furtived out of eye corner. Madison relax you preach the moment's maximization among all your preachings enjoy here's Lucy real love uninhibited no problems of tradition tradition Fran or limited environment Jeanine this intense lovely warm zestful girl revolted against her wealth good stuff is swinging with you oh this is it.

"You're so affectionate. I love people who're affectionate," I confessed.

"I do, too," she smiled radiant we held hands across the table and kissed lightly softly quickly a hundred times. We sat back, our face shining, we still holding hands, what happens now what's the next thing should leave the Kiwi sitting here tightening something always snatches joy take it take it while ye may for blooms quickly cut and buds better than headless stems—

"Let's go walk," I said.

"All right."

Outside glittercold late January placarded its large stars above Houston Street and we pressed against seized each other by the bus stop sign unable to move any further from the Kiwi. Hesitation. Time passing. Speak up she nestled against me don't let this pass away.

"Come home with me."

She looks at me what seems a long slow minute. Come on spontaneous uninhibited affectionate liberated free free like me Lucy and don't damp this soaring flame moth fly in with me who cares what morrow brings.

"You really want me to don't you?"

"Yes. Yes. Yes." We cover each other's face with kisses. Alright show on the road gently turn her around and we lifting our legs in slow together time move off.

She moaned moaned limp, abandoned to her comes and more she moaned and gasped fuller stronger I became inspired to travel on and on but finally the now ticked and I forgot her and myself went black/blind that little space when all happens of itself fires on struggle to attain again and again and by memory/fantasy when not in real.

We kissed and kissed and she turned to sleep, I too, but soon woke and had joyous light, turned her to me now really fire every particle of her seemed love/divine/Aphrodite Grecian splendor saltwave marble columns/skin fluid hairs spit tan white underneaths read lower lips Lucy years effort what holds back even with Fran somewhat now anything goes totally yours lover/worshipper/dance all yours, I tongued her swabbing gums reaching back to palate, fingers reveling on skin hair and into fluid.

She pushed me, eyes frightened, "What're you doing?"

"What am I doing?" Incredulous.

"Let me sleep. You frighten me."

"I frighten you?"

"Please. You were so good. Let me sleep." Wide eyes stare, her hands pressed palm up against my chest.

I sit up astounded, things below begin to clutch, I feel vast moving inside inchoate clouding. "So good! Then why— My God, Lucy!" I fumble at her again.

"Please. Please."

"But never, Lucy. I swear to you, never the first time so good, we can do so much, how can I stop, you don't know what you do to me—"

Slowly she sits up. The blankets fall to our waists and we both sit up. She folds her arms, each hand holding an opposite elbow, her breasts frail but stronger than my strength.

"Let's talk it out," she said. "This is very important. Let's talk it out very carefully."

"Talk it out! What's there to talk out? We have the most splendid loving and suddenly you're cold as ice, what's happening, why don't you just relax?" Relax myself, too excited, but what's with her my spontaneous other truly free one, women can go on and on, it's man who generally can't keep up who ever heard of a healthy women who couldn't take a man long as he lasted well yeah her and her and her didn't but complex man/woman getting to bed complex to really make it big but how in tortuous earth hell can it stay complex after you've really come together?

"I had a very hard childhood—" she begins.

"Don't replay your psychoanalysis now," I shout tone down Joe tone down.

"If it's important to you, we should talk it out very carefully and to do that we have to understand."

Her cool pleasant voice hammered hail my wheat headed out beaten flat.

"Goddamit, I don't understand how you could have been so hot and good and now worse than a frightened virgin I don't care what happened to you when you were six or two or in your mother's womb."

She put one hand on my shoulder. "I don't understand it all either, but you must believe that it will work out. I've been trying for a long time with all I can and what we had was my fullest surrender I've ever made but you came at me while I was sleeping and the old terrible things must have reacted and filled my mind again." Voice patient as to a spoiled child. She must be very tired why do I keep pestering undignified posture almost like begging.

"I understand," my voice sounded stiff scrub oak in the wind.

"I don't think a woman should sleep with a man, even her husband unless she wants to—" we slipped down under the covers and I held her, her last phrase sounded like a threat. Was I supposed to rouse myself find out if she deigned or not subject to what unknown forces and never bother her delicate psyche if slightly out-of-whack but only turn against myself maybe sometimes delicate psyche too and say down boy and myself swallow all repression what in hell did women think men made of had to be ideal sensitive understanding full of control yet proud passionate unreserved on top, what about *my* ideal that sensual steaming earth always open to the plow springing for the always new and restoring fruits always ready with response to hardened treasured skills and strength bringing home so proudly spears and flags trophies of Holy Lands to adorn/inspire beloved and buy her priests to pleasure that part of her soul man has no real need of and not only that but just at times give up whatever vulgar probe my fingers tongue or prick desired.

Slowly relaxed to sleep chuckling finally remembering Lucy's hose somehow from her sturdy tramping energetic legs always twisted loose around the knee she didn't really buy them long enough she pulled them off with intense practical gesture like farm women at end of full day no coquetry and yet it made her seem so fragile/precious because she wore them anyway though sheer effect all lost and must be hell of a strain for independent girl to do all that woman business, old Lucy sure about the fastest undresser in the business, no nonsense there, and pretty spunky her sitting up to talk carefully to hard-on passionate madman ready to take off and walk hurt and lonely and freeze in that bitter cold glitter old January night on some vacant lot to imagine stoic compensations trying to make out Orion through Manhattan haze how useless all efforts are yes how much better still here under warm blankets holding warm her, listening to slightly chuffing lips.

26

"What I like about you, Joe, is you're always looking for the truth," Bill Layton said as we coffee lingered at the Hip Bagel jazz listening eyeing occasionally the newest Village-seeking waitress trim legs and large gold earrings. An aspiring artist from Queens by the name of Lita Chayevsky.

"And never finding though it's all about us–like a fish looking for water." Not truth but most life-enhancing theory, insights, lies, who cares what. "Sometimes I think we were better off out West," I said. "What do we do here? I go through girl after girl and you work away on your damned inventions. Where's it getting us?"

"I'll make my pile and retire in Sante Fe in three or four years and do Indian studies."

"With a devoted wife and raise your kids."

"Right."

"In a way I wish I could dream of that."

"Some day you'll find her."

"Her. Her! Christ, whaddya mean her? The aim in life can't be to find some woman to be all end all bring everything home to. Love just don't last. We both tried it, didn't we?"

"Yeah." I shouldn't have said it, breaking up a marriage never fun.

"Of course you want children–"

"Yeah. I really do. And I want to be young enough to

understand them when they grow up."

"You're already too old if you were a parent. Besides, grandfolks are best my grandfolks were best wait till you're fifty-five or sixty and have kids and you'll treat 'em right."

"Well, my father was too old to go tramping with me when I was sixteen and I missed it."

"Everybody loves their grandparents. Think, if you wait you can die when the kids are twenty-one and you won't be in their way and they'll all think of you fondly."

"But then nobody would ever have grandparents."

"Yeah, but it'd slow the whole world up one generation of procreation and solve the overpopulation problem as well."

Bill lit him a cigarette.

"I don't want children." I said.

"Maybe you will someday."

"Don't think so. I always wanted to do something great. Plato: men who can't have spiritual children want those of the flesh."

"I'd like both—but then I don't know this great bit that drives you—I want to produce some new chemicals, put together my book on the Indians and dandle grandchildren on my knee."

Sometimes you can't even talk with your best friend, your true brother, you don't know what to say.

"Sometimes I can even talk with you Bill, I don't know what to say, I don't know what I'm looking for, I try to live each moment to full as if it were last but statistically probable others will follow each demanding its full, I want to see everything, do everything--William Blake had a little drawing of a man standing on earth putting a big pole out toward the moon, I want, I want —that's me I recognized it when I saw it eighteen fourteen no now fifteen years ago and I've never changed but I'm always changing I can't finish sentences anymore because I've changed between subject and predicate my predicated subject becomes object of my subjective verb gerunding into noun and sometimes I think everything we say's only ejaculation you have to listen to tone and look at eyes and even then who knows what's in that flesh blood electronic hive or even if what's in there has anything to do with weight mass total gland regulated or upset growing from a sperm/ova collision regardless of any want or idea into man or woman and then old age and ending, who can stop or change a jot and little of real destiny no matter what we think about it, except for suicide-type freedom year–"

"Wish I had a tape recorder when you're hot."

Flattered, tattered, suspicious, I shot him a glance but didn't comment years ago I read reread shouted Burke Churchill Lincoln Demosthenes Pericles (Thucydides version) to mankind womankind out there and I at such a moment then and there producing honor glory rage exaltation in their/my breasts standing off threatening hosts and building building–what?

"I used to dream of an America Athens with no slaves because machines did it all except maybe two/three years a man would put in doing the unprogrammable type labor good for his back and balls and soul anyway, architecture soaring curving swooping, grapes and orchards ponds trails forest parks everywhere, laboratories where one could enter and work to solve what problems interested, guitars and dancing in the streets, men and women and boys and girls who could love each other and old men and old women white haired earthy and beautiful who watched counseled remembered, Indians, Negroes, Orientals, and whites a color symphony of human variations and no man but would have tried them all, poems and speeches chanted in the squares and we *would* have squares with coffee shops and people could smoke marijuana too or anything else they pleased besides just benzedrine and tranquilizers, and you'd only pick up cars at citys' edges within which we'd walk superbly gowned conversing with our friends on love and art and knowledge of stars metals earth's core and time before history began and time when history shall cease and whatever other cabbage/king dialectic nonsequitor ad hominem logical or any other scenes of words that shall amuse/instruct/inspire/provoke response, oh from shining sea to sea life-blessed brothers/sisters all we should each arc our way still difficult and dangerous enough because Nature preserves but three salmon from each five thousand eggs to full growth and why assume Nature's less prodigal perhaps more prodigal with us so far spendrift tossed furthest, at least on this suburban star's planet, no shallow dream for optimists this" Lucy's turning from me in the night yes love most arduous creativity Haephestus himself would flinch at such task trying to secure Aphrodite from arrant onsets, "but all that only minimum platform for these soul struggles which would be perhaps fiercest in all creation fiercer than Tamerlane or shark, killing wounding souls of which we should each be as indeed we now are but even more so then vast multitudes, societies indeed, and one man in his time would play a million parts double and triple leveled, tiered like Asiatic quinquiremes bearing down splendored in their fleets to extend their worlds and hundreds of millions of universes should glow radiate around this land and indeed recognize their fellow galaxy systems throughout this globe and signal exuberant hellos throughout the worlds of space and hell, man, we'd all jubilate."

I loved Bill. I could try anything with him and let it take me where it willed. He never balked.

"Crazy," he said.

We called for our check and debated the tip to give the new pert waitress and decided to "break her in right."

27

I looked in the mirror still thirty-three year old bullnecked smooth faced no later Rembrandt wrinkled torment wings of soul brooding no matter how kinked convulted twisted grey matter behind, in the boarding house in Houston Texas no air conditioning then last year of World War woke up in late morning pools of sweat couldn't get off swing shift though but that's what I fifteen-year-old loved, reality holding so tight I couldn't escape could always fly so easy sought out the hardest traps anyway the two medical students in room next paraded like a loaf of bread something to the dining table where Mrs. Riarty always said don't gulp your food Joe there's plenty this is not ordinary boarding house where they starve you and glared around daring any to deny, the two med students called me, "Joe want a look?" hefting Riarty's footlong black and yellow bone-handed carving knife sliced off a thin piece handed it to me be careful with it but rubbery seemed strange enough "do you know what that is, no, well that's a human brain and we're slicing it up like a loaf of bread" they laughed and I laughed and we started dancing around the table a loaf of bread a loaf of bread and the funny thing the slice I held in my hand smooth and not full of little turdlike hardnesses at all but smooth solid rubbery very peaceful thing to hold.

Upbeat alright those first days of February and I cheerful

because seemed resurrection and hadn't really had to die at all and at 'em hit 'em again harder harder come on team let's go at Elkhorn they'd finally pushed a touchdown over the last 30 seconds after we'd led them all the way, they won 20-14, rated number two in the State but we were better, on this scoring play they'd pushed to our 3 yard line last down they had to make it or we won we all knew they were coming over right tackle where Lennie just couldn't quite hack it big guy but not quite fighter enough and I at guard and Dave at end both made slight charge forward just in case then veered to Lennie's hole but because not quite faith and we hadn't gone there right off their big left half already at line of scrimmage and we lunged backward to catch his ankles but full outstretched he fell across the white and it was Coach's last year he wanted to beat Elkhorn more than anyone "old Ramsey they call me" he'd said in the huddle before the game "they say that I've outlived my time" we still used Knute Rockne's spin formation all of us knew the T was better, technology moves football too in USA always better sharper but Ramsey'd won a state championship ten years before incredible in a school so small and desperately we labored to move those old plays every opposition coach knew by heart "and maybe I have but this is my last year I didn't want to tell you that before but it's time for a younger man, and I don't like a lot of sentimental talk, you know that, and this is first and only thing I've ever asked you go out and beat Elkhorn for old Ramsey you can do it you can be the best team I ever had better yes than '35" and we roared and in eight minutes 14-0 and believe we could have made it 30-0 but old Ramsey gave us orders to defend the lead take no risks to strike for more use our exceptional defense and I drew down on us one disastrous penalty that helped them make their first six and all my tackles most I believe I ever made in one game not enough atonement later and waiting for their last kickoff knowing we'd have to run it back all the way to win forlorn chance because the whistle'd blow, tears down our faces, we'd missed what playing three years together we'd known we could do our senior year namely make it all the way how many hours weeks months we'd trained planned dreamed and there we stood forlorn rage grief tears game for that last try and blocking as best we could helped Damon run it back to their forty we'd have scored in four or five but that was it, time ran out, and we walked off after first of course congratulating an Elkhorn opposite and especially all of us their goddam passer we'd knocked down again and again but he'd kept them moving moving moving and old Ramsey and all of us mea culpa the lights stood bent over the deserted field chill November no longer bracing but wintry and we spike clattered into our hot showers and Damon said "I never knew just what we'd lost till I looked over at Kickoff and saw Joe Madison crying and then I knew what we'd done and I wanted to run it all the way back but I just couldn't get any further I did my best" and we all or I at least thought we did our best and somebody Dave or me or Lennie or all of us shouted Well we'll win the conference anyway and we roared and crowded out hungry to eat steaks and revel in post mortems.

That early February upbeat and Joe Madison cat on his feet always lands upright victory from defeat or even defeated transcends by moving to higher level oh dialectic abolition of disaster diabolic with life lure but lure's the stuff of traps, anyway Bill Layton and I started up a chemistry lab just South of the Village in an old abandoned loft and we dreamed of fortunes, small but adequate for our philosophical needs, certainly providing many mountain trips, and Lucy who'd quit college and been through the goddam mill more my seething chaos' mate than Fran but Fran and I hadn't quite exchanged the final letters yet and so that still a possibility and Jeanine friendlier again I liked my fun where found but believed also in long relationships, and down at Worldwide Rufus and I searched modus vivendi. I was not born for failure, immortal bird, the self-same wit that bears thee on made euphoria and dawn, Joe Madison out of a life spree, Alcibiades in Athens dazzled by his brilliance, in Sparta amazed by his fortitude and diligence, in

Persia astounded by his grandiosity and sexual aptitude, all colors like chameleon but philosophy's white, well, Joe Madison could even philosophize.

So in December when Rufus called me in could see something was astir. First let's face it, I thought, angry.

"I don't guess you liked the report much." He hadn't commented on it at all.

"No. I found it a mass of stylistic incongruities with no clear recommendations." Very deliberate and definite.

"Well, my real report was in here to you," I said, "and I could see you didn't think anything of it." Hot under the collar no father now an old man with red cheeks sagging purple lines and I with young strong body future all ahead whatever distinction why should I fear or even be kind nobody pushed me around I could fight back.

"Joe, someday, you'll understand that presentation is very important. You're young, bright, maybe even as bright as you think you are." The old bastard kept a sharp knife too I chuckled inside I liked an open fight no dark emotions but intellect out there flashing, "but you get wrapped up in your subject and the rest of us maybe not quite as bright need a little explanation as to how you've arrived at your interesting conclusions, but you explode it out so fast that it's difficult to follow your reasoning and I—who have to keep many things on my mind besides your project—" Chalk two Rufus you're in rare form "become irritated and you become irritated at my irritation and very little's achieved."

Excellent analysis why do you keep getting irritated then, boring as some versions of hell to go A-B-C-D I like intuitive leaps gestating gestalts beholds! I and mine convince by our presence let arguers babble on. "Well, " I said, "I'll try to remember to spell out the small details. Sometimes," in a very modest quiet tone, "I hate to inflict a repetition of what's already been said."

"Nobody can remember everything, Joe, remember that."

The order tone had barked through Rufus A-1 exponent of

democracy, so pleased with any small triumph I superiorly, "Yes, *sir.*"

"Anyway, I called you in to talk about something different."

*

Actually striding along streets looking into sunny windows not into just pretending but at me reflection could see all beginning lines and sags what made all those tiny cells finally groove and then collapse?

By sort of mutual consent it seemed I stayed away from Iran except for occasional analysis of some specific, but Kennedy president after ten years of nothing doing in the States except get the Communists whom the FBI finally became the biggest financial contributors to and of course the always Get Richer slogans, and times at least to flux again and Rufus began to Look Back Toward America, dream foal of the open range.

And I fired up, "The Rocky Mountains," I said, "the Rockies! There's a treasure house underneath the scrabbled gopher holes the early miners scratched. Sure, the increasing depth, the long tough winters, the development of cheap mines around the world under colonial rule, all this made ghost towns even though the walnut bars and diamond dust mirrors survive here and there, good places to drink a beer by the way, but with rise of nationalism around the world, end of empires, higher wages, automation's advance here in USA and tools to conquer winter, the Rockies, Rufus, are really it—a company that moves in now—with the proper vision and far reaching public oriented plans—gains the ground floor and can build from New Mexico to Canada."

"Step by step," Rufus said. "Remember, Joe, one step at a time and that's how things that last are built," a slow grave smile, "if there's really building done."

So I'd wound up involved again in a project for profit and no dream/Utopia transformations of social world, but what the hell, now I'd roll and go commute New York and the Frontier and culture brains and brawn the Union one and forever labor and capital land and dollar dream and dynamite and there among the mountain meadows old revered founder of cities Joe Madison and Bill Layton retired ranching looking at the skies with their radio telescope a summer university for wandering youth with fire in its eye and in the long evenings memories of cliffs hammers striking sparks from breaking rocks the daring inferences from this prosaic operation conjoining with contours of a given granite ledge to produce a better base for all humanity's tower—or at any rate cheaper lead, zinc, silver, alchemist of mountains, I bent again my shoulder to the wheel, drew my cheeks with some good conscience, and tried to forget why I'd originally laughed at Heirs, Inc., and gone to work for Rufus Brown.

28

Things fairly upbeat then and we'd planned to drive to Washington Lucy and I, yes four days away from New York's wham wham would do us good only I fell sick.

I never fell sick except almost died of pneumonia when I was six one morning I awoke "I want *Post's Forty Per Cent Bran Flakes*" and my father sitting by side of bed leaned over and kissed me his lips pressed out and wet a real kiss I couldn't understand why he was crying the sheets so clean and fresh and smooth and warm the nurse rushed in smiling and before I'd finished my bowl they'd put in pure cream my mother appeared and such an air of joy I was never so happy I ate *Post's Forty Per Cent Bran Flakes* every morning and sometimes for dessert at supper for years afterward and nobody including myself ever understood why "It tastes so good," I always said and I used to wonder why people ever died of pneumonia all I could rememeber of it that morning not bad when I was nine my father huge abstraction whom I avoided one had handed official size envelope inside which two single-spaced typed sheet the top of first one bearing the title "Letters of a Father to his Son" and he said "Here's something for you," and I took with suspicion, sure it loaded with a lot of bull part of it said when you were smaller I watched and prayed over you all night we thought you were going to die of pneumonia and I thought yeah likely story what's prayer got to do with anything you mumble it over every dinner and does it ever do anything and at Grandmother's it only holds up the dinner because I was there when you weren't and till he died last year I never saw Granddad have any dinner prayer except when you were there he just dived right in and ate he always held his fork ready in his right hand while you were praying at least you did make short ones the second you finished he speared him a piece of bread and took a big bite broke out grinning a good noises and confusion everybody filled their plates and ate and if that's what you were doing over me what do I care you were thinking of your god you should have been thinking of me and it doesn't do any good anyway at nine I'd already said goodbye to all that.

In Junior high I wore a T-shirt barearmed to school in December and January my mother "you're going to catch your death of cold" I never saw anybody die of a cold "You'll get pheumonia" she said I always laughed Joe Madison against the elements at home in this seahowling world later wished I had blonde hair blue eyes Viking prow into the unknown really surprised when one girl looked at my eyes real close "you have beautiful eyes" "what do you mean" I said "they change colors brown green hazel" but they're not blue hard icy universe mastering I cried to myself you lie they're not really beautiful they're soft brown and doglike anyway my mother really irritated me she developed a refrain over and over "you think you're so strong, Joe, you're so proud of your strength, but sometimes I don't think you're really so strong you can get sick, too, like other people remember that pneumonia" actually I think she did once in a while scare me a little bit of course I kept wearing only the T-shirt though I had to run to school and play violently to stay warm at all finally when my friend John completely gave up and wore a heavy jacket then in January I went over and wore something but for years I never really dressed warm in fact it's still a struggle.

I held it against Lucy that I fell sick because I'd had to leave for Out West to look at some possible mines just after our first two days and I came back soon as I could but it was two weeks before I charged off the jet to pay phone and dialed. Her answering service "oh yes, Mr. Madison, it's you. She said call at —' I did. "Lucy, I'm back! I'll taxi right in. Meet me at home, huh?"

"Joe, why don't you come to my place?" Goddam it, she never kept it in order and people all her friends ex-lovers acquaintances always calling she knew everybody at least a representative type in the world I wanted her at my place where I refused telephone and we could be uninterrupted, two weeks I'd longed for her daily of course most of the day absorbed in geology but at nights I longed for except generally pretty tired quickly to sleep but for a few seconds/minutes I fantasied nearly always her naturally some changes for variety but now back rambunctious raring to go why didn't she come to my place?

"You sure you'd rather that than coming over?"

"Yes, Joe, please."

Finally, after sufficient silence to indicate displeasure. "Okay."

The taxi got lost and it was an hour before I arrived. Why doesn't she live in the Village instead of out here in Cobble Heights, that Brooklyn tangle seemed more remote provincial than the Rocky Mountains, pushed my western hat back, set down my suitcase, rapped her door, she appeared, snub nose shining eyes I picked her up leaned back against the wall and I don't know how long we held that way.

Lying in her bed she asleep and knowing now that one good time a night all she could take right now but I not asleep I softly held and loved intertwined with her she'd left a window open and the cold damp penetrated her covers I got cold lay over half of her and stroked the rest to keep her warm didn't want to wake her to ask for cover or close the window I wore T-shirts to school all year almost and certainly healthy from two mountain weeks Joe Madison invulnerable "Not as strong as you think" I'm stronger than *you* think and finally the sweat all over me disappeared and the worst cold left and made it to sleep for a while late in the morning.

Thursday night I told her, "damn it, Lucy, I'm feeling like hell, but I'm sure we can leave tomorrow morning."

"I hope so." I thought she meant only she hoped she could escape the City for four days. It's your fault, if you hadn't kept the window open or I hadn't been so fearful of your sensitivity I'd just up and closed it anyway I hoped sick I'd not ruin her expectations, she'd really built up hopes for this trip, me too.

Friday fever soared I just couldn't do it Lucy came over and we tried to laugh and joke but she worried I could tell my being sick depressed her she sat dutifully around the apartment.

"Why don't you go on home. I don't like people around when I'm sick anyway." Please stay I only want to see if you really want to stay.

She didn't really want to stay she struggled "I can't leave you, Joe, you're pretty sick. Besides I can read and we can talk when you feel like it." Don't pity me, Lucy, I don't need it. Joe Madison can always survive tough as an old prospector in his desert shack bushy-eyebrowed downing Rum and sweating it out old prospectors outlived others for whatever it was worth and each new spring they grizzled into cold mountain streams panning for El Dorado, just love me love me for whatever I am unconditionally and forever hold me kiss me though I'm a fevered wreck and not much youth left now and you eleven years younger why should you risk illness contamination because of what mutually projected fictions that brought us here in this apartment among the sooty-millions two brief atoms in the black world how in God's name did the Saints kiss lepers when I first walked down Chicago's West Madison Street a grey-haired head lay on the street a foot from my toes, snot ran down one three or four day unshaven cheek, the mouth opened, white froth lay on purple lips, blood from a gash on his head had frozen on the dirty snow, I stood there looking down for Christsakes pick him up wipe the blood off see if he's alive call somebody a blue-jeaned denim-jacketed potbellied fellow tapped me on the shoulder Come on you better leave the cops find you here you'll spend the night in jail answering questions they might even frame you good they don't like your looks, everybody likes Joe Madison's looks but that's out West maybe here they don't and I let him pull me away from that awful head. Who deserved anyone making a sacrifice for them, nobody really sacrificed for anybody, and pseudo-making sacrifices they build around you prison, stifling, misery, obligations, you couldn't escape, people wanted, and who could blame them, something a lot back for pseudo-sacrifice because otherwise it would become sacrifice.

"Go on home, Lucy, don't be a martyr. I'm sorry I fucked up your weekend."

"Joe, will you shut up? I'm staying with you. I'm worried about you." She kissed me oh how much I liked it and fell off to sleep.

At midnight Saturday felt like something stabbing my eye. Pain sharp. I winced my face contorted don't scream Spartan Stoic Indian Godalmighty it hurt grit teeth fingernails in palms, sweat, straighten legs, flex toes, all the tricks, again and again the pain daggered my eye tears started running out I had to moan Lucy I thought please don't think I'm trying for attention I can't help it this sonofabitch hurts I can't help making a noise oh yeah Joe couldn't you really stand it a little more those guys under the Gestapo didn't some of them, human body can only stand so much pain then it blacks out last till then fuck the theory did those bastards ever take torture I let a strange noise out between my teeth startling even myself.

"Joe!" Lucy rolled off the couch and stood frantic-eyed above the bed.

"I can't help it. It hurts."

She made wild contradictory motions with her hands.

"Don't worry, Lucy, it'll go away," I hope to hell but another sound strangled out.

"You've got to go to the hospital," she said.

I argued but we dressed because the goddam thing wouldn't

stop hurting.

Outside large flakes of soft wet snow. As far up as I could see with my one good eye swirling softly wind swaying flakes all different they say because no one man's seen two alike and maybe so the air warmer than day before because each gram of snow flicking off its hundred calories of heat as the active liquid molecules gave up the struggle and settled down to solid already three inches deep on the sidewalk and couldn't hear the noise of a single car intense silence on New York and all the concrete winter prairies, "My God, Lucy," I couldn't move, "how beautiful."

"Oh," she laughed exasperation, "you idiot!"

We hiked off through the wintry wastes she said, "Maybe we can get a taxi on Houston Street or Fourth Street," but I didn't think we could and gloated at the walk though the pain seized me every twenty/thirty steps maybe the cold and snow will freeze it out damn doctors who knows about the human body?

At the emergency ward they wouldn't let Lucy go in with me, they consigned her without a thought to a shitgreen sofa in a waiting room otherwise all brown and grey and led me off to sign my name and other sundries finally sitting me on a stool in a cold room naked to the waist, "wait for the doctor."

Four men, two of them cops, lugged in, straight-jacketed, the handsomest man I'd ever seen, at least six-feet-four, pure white skin at least two hundred twenty proportioned pounds, all he had was shorts, blue eyes, blonde reddish hair, superb Irish male. They dropped him down on a table.

"Took eight men to bring him down," the cop flung to the intern. "He tore a whole bar apart, had six men knocked to the floor." Nobody else said anything. Everyone stared at the man who might have been a god. His eyes stared towards the ceiling and only his belly moved from breathing.

One interne, plumpish, glassed, pulled a chair to the man's head and began to talk. "Do you remember how it started?" Silence. "Do you feel any special pain?" Silence. "We're friends here. What's your name?" Silence.

In front of me stretched out on another table also stripped to his shorts breathing with snorty chokes an unconscious man whose chest rose up like a mountain above the cavern of his still hard belly though he bald and domed with a crag, his nose smashed almost flat snubbed and snaked from eyebrow ridge to above his scabbed upper lip his ears gnarled like ancient tree trunks his legs surprisingly graceful for his gorilla chest and shoulders his knees almost Michelangelo's Christ's and toward this hulk advanced a poised interne wheeling a boxlike machine with many knobs and windows. The interne delicately tuned knobs to his satisfaction, one window glowed green, and he began reeling out tiny wires carefully pasting them on the choking hulk. Slowly and precisely, two under each arm, two on the neck, two on the forehead he labored for more than a hour spinning his web while the green window glowed.

A small trim Black entered collar turned backward wearing black and the two nurses standing at the door ignored him they were joking with an old fat drunk trying to tie his shoes, "Now Mr Hartley," the plump one giggled, "you be good now and don't let's find you here next week." The fat drunk looked up his eyes watery his lips drooping as if to grin like an ancient custom required to all blathering slithering off his back then panting hoarsely returned to his struggle with his shoe laces almost obscured below a vast protuberance.

Off to my right just below the feet of the hulk an adolescent in red monkey uniform of some hotel sat dangling a bandaged finger over a porcelain bowl open-mouthed staring at the nurses a goodlooking guy and tall nurse smiled at him from time to time. "Hey," I said quietly as I could for some reason or no reason "your finger's dripping blood right through that bandage." The porcelain bowl had blood in it looked a quarter-inch deep.

"Oh," he said, "well, I have been here an hour."

"Well, why don't you have the nurse bandage your finger right?"

"It's cut off at the tip," he said.

"Hey, nurse," I called, "why don't you re-bandage this guy's finger?"

Nobody else seemed to look but she did grimacing angrily and then walked over and rebandaged the dripping finger.

The trim small Black had pulled out a little bible and he slowly walked around the hulk not looking at anything it seemed except after reading some words he'd place some water with fingertips in a little cross-like motion at intervals on the hulk. When he reached the place where he had to pass between me and the hulk, there was only a foot, he still didn't even look at me, I stared hard as I could, and fractionally his eyes seemed to dart to their farthest corner as to catch a peripheral glance but then he returned totally lost in his task never so far as I saw even peeping at the face of the hulk. The interne ignored his presence and so did the nurses. He vanished from the room.

After two hours I got tired of sitting there. My eye pain had become only throb. The one interne now had his hand on the beautiful man's shoulder still talking low and soft to him, the other studied his glowing green and made marks in his notebook.

"Hey, " I said to the one on the machine, "I'm leaving, but why don't you tie up this guy's finger?"

"Oh, " he said, "Are you all right now?"

"Well, a lot better."

"Look," he said, "I'll do you a favor. I'll go with you to the window and sign No Treatment on your slip, that'll save you your two bucks."

"Thanks," I said. The bastard had a heart. Madison aren't you sorry you jump to such black conclusions about the human race.

29

Last night here in Marrakesh a dream.

Running through drizzling grey rain warm rain descending at a contact angle thirty degrees from normal against my face running trying to reach the station in time to greet the train chugging bellowing in the valley below a great herd of red horses stampeded from a side road in front of me down toward ocean shore, upon meeting the train two girls one blonde one brunette descended only the blonde spoke she had a broad fleshy back bare, when she turned from me I could see the hang of her loose large breasts on one side the shadows under the smock front I'm frightened she said a pasty-faced guy tried to touch and muss me on the train he said I'm going to the same place you're going and I'll have you there the three of us sprawled down the cliff to the ocean beach walking underneath the dark shadow of the cantilevered black iron railway station everything lonely and deserted she turned to me they say there're a lot of guys like that in this town it's an old beach town salt grass broken windows broken-down cots with rusty springs they'll probably all jump on us you'll save us won't you the hell I will I thought frightened but not up to turning back, if they jump you it's your fault I'm not pushing you there it's your own free will maybe if there's only one guy I'll fight him if I think can lick him but if he's got a knife or gun he can have you to hell with dying for you dogs started barking behind oh that explains the horses a fox hunt wonderful red stallions must be wonderful to hunt down foxes one of the dogs jumped and bit my hand no not me I cried the other dogs gleaming teeth bore down five in all and circled a second jumped and I swung two in the air but when all others jumped and bit they'd bring me down the blood would finally spout they'd go wild rend and chew me to bits come back I called to the girls now at least a hundred yards away walking to their own doom come back come help but why should they add to the dogs' destruction let them find their own the other dogs prepared to jump I'm going to die come back come back come help I screamed at the two disappearing figures knowing they wouldn't shouldn't come I prepared to experience fangs.

"Did they fix you up?" Lucy snapped awake from her head lolling pose when I touched her shoulder.

"No. Lots of guys worse off, so I decided I'm not dying why take up their time. It's only throbbing now."

She stood up furious. "You're not leaving till they look at you, Joe, you were in terrible pain. It might start again, you can't tell."

I grinned. "Don't grin, Joe, you're always smiling and grinning. Take care of yourself."

Why didn't she like my grin, genial Joe, a good grin. "I'm sure it's stopped," after all the universe had no reason to persecute, I liked it, at home in all its aspects.

"I sat here worrying about you. They wouldn't tell me anything. They wouldn't let me go into see you, I just had to sit out here in this nightmare and worry."

"You finally got some sleep," I said letting just a drop of acid fall.

"Oh, Joe! The last two minutes I might have dozed, I'm exhausted."

"Well, let's get out into the snow!" my head felt light and airy at last escape that misery inside I couldn't wait to be away.

Lucy shrugged, outside five inches deep the flakes swayed down lower larger. Even on Sixth Avenue nothing moved one cabby poking a flashlight under the hood his car almost inch deep under white, "Can't you take us home," Lucy cried out.

"Come on," I said angry she didn't also love the snow but slogged a small furry creature in scuffing boots head down.

"Lady," he said, "I don't think I can get myself home."

Washington Park seemed almost a forest I pulled Lucy by the arm to hike around its paths, "Look, look" I pointed here and there everywhere seemed noteworthy why didn't she swing, palpitate to probity?

"Let's get home, Joe, you're sick and I'm tired."

How could she be tired I was sick temperature 102 throbbing head I should be tired Joe Madison rises above circumstance death only that mother fucker shall conquer.

"Allright goddam it alright!" we slogged our way through the cold on home, our faces reddened and chilled if not to the bone at least on every inch of flesh except maybe right under the arms and crotch. She climbed in bed with me forgetting about catching flu or too cold to care and I too selfish to care we dropped to sleep no particularly tenderness but just blanket rounded shrouded bare ass naked seeking WARM SLEEP and end to all difficulty.

Two o'clock the next afternoon we finally stirred my nose needed only one good blow head clearer and hot for Lucy. I felt overcome by a strange desire I couldn't control it, "Let's do it in the shower," I said placing her hands.

Oh Christ, don't argue, Lucy just do please it's very important why can't you wait Joe a week or two play it easy she's fighting her way to relax with you. "It just seems important. It'll be good, really. I'll be very good with you."

She prepared her diaphragm while I danced into the shower carefully adjusted water to good and warm "You like it warm, don't you?"

"Almost hot," she said.

"Good."

She appeared face around the curtain uncertain she stepped in after only a second's hesitation. We soaped each back and forth and slid together our smooth surfaces I never more ready to go "How?" she asked. I turned her around and, feeling her flow, tremendously gloried in full thrust one hand on each fair cheek and just sailing forth on slow luxurious in/out ride she straightened up I fell out, "Joe, I can't, here, I'm afraid of the water the diaphragm'll leak, let's go to bed –"

Roars howls within for once for once only can't you just let me be and rollick Other just once in total tune with me why such difficulty is so much to ask/dream not to be crossed for say one time must one solid hour straight wish fulfillment. "Look, I'll withdraw, don't worry." I pushed at small of her back trying to bend her down again softly gently loverlike not too hard she ought to be so hot she couldn't stop how can she no at time like this.

"I can't" she said, "I'd worry too much, I just know the water'll get in and leak around the edges and I don't want to be pregnant."

"I don't want you pregnant either," I said.

She turned fully around, I wilted, how in hell call this love, why can't do without it, "I'll go to the bed," she said, "why don't you finish your shower and then come to me."

"Ga-a-ah" I choked out "Okay! Okay!"

After a couple minutes cooling off I joined her under our covers which we threw off and it turned out very well indeed, "We're really beginning to love each other," I said, she nodded, and exhausted I fell asleep again luxuriating in the sweat pouring from me that's good for fevers to sweat a lot.

At four she woke me. "Joe, I'm running to Landau's for three or four hours to help him on his manuscript." I jerked totally awake Landau her awakening father love mentor allright cool it Joe you know this girl's life like your own many-peopled many needs she made it clear you said OK that both you lived as well you pleased you wouldn't have it any other way.

"Okay," I said, "have a good session."

She walked out with her suitcase, we kissed briefly at the door, and I lay down again.

*

What possessed me that late afternoon and night—sickness revulsion fury despair all the devils of a lifetime danced and shrieked I rose from my bed stalked my rooms did exercises flailing arms peered into the mirror lifted my eyelids actually screamed cried even kicked at my blankets like a child I forgot for a while even any bric-a-brac of my layered images pain from where everywhere my sickness my lack of strength the working again to make profits involvement with bankers I didn't know what I wanted I hated social systems tore up the *New York Times* Lucy left, shredded it on the floor never read a newspaper again Thoreau "always the same news" that a hundred twenty years ago two per cent of my life wasted on newspapers all of it some reporter's idea outside anyhow of whatever's happening about what sells, the retractions always small print page thirty-seven my God what hadn't I studied desperately to know to understand crazy star wheeling forever expanding unless cyclic contracting but what's eternity infinity Palomar doesn't reach to end of stare even radio telescope I mean the same plain kind of stars as sun how about universes negative matter or non-dimensions outside our ken who knows Bill and long talk with old Marsala beating his deerskin drum drinking red wine about the Indian ways they brought rain and Marsala beat his drum with mighty blows after showing his foxskins belts headdress and silver we walked later through the silent adobe houses stars silent trees silent we silent I nearly died I could hardly breathe silence after that mighty drum and talk of magic while we lounged a band of three exploring strange notions and all of that to die television cars young men to pass it on to and what lasts mothers grow old frail and die never transfixed by the true point of our need and I have raged among men and women and among my selves except once drunk on bottle of red wine lying all night on a desert gully awake there maybe a few other times and those long ago. Loafing, disreputable, I lay among grandfather's hogs soaking in green mud wallows summer sun hot hot grunting and rolling slowly side to side with white snooted hogs stroking in the cattle tank and forever through the windmills creak of invisible wind why don't you just give up remember the peyote just sit down behind all the benches right in the path why don't you just stop just give up just see what happens stop pushing raging planning calculating lusting loving maybe none of that whole circus show drama's you what's the actor really like can you face yourself Joe can you forget your name Joe Madison forget bright baubled pictures and see what actually wells up when no push Jeanine's Dakota Swedish friend who I'd acrobatically fucked a couple of nights said you're a big ship all sails outstretched scudding ten knots an hour faster than the wind why don't you turn off the engine?

Lucy had walked out on me. Everything focussed. Why she'd taken her suitcase. Sick and tired of a sick madman spoiled bourgeois bitch never had she really loved me just a big black fuck Fran had said laughing tentatively you remind me of a big Black in context I'd swelled a bit but that's not love at all let the going get a little rough Lucy's off the Papa Landau brilliant long nosed old bastard fought with Chinese guerrillas in '38 coming out of Soviet breaking new paths studying primeval psychologic levels sensual not earthy subtle laboring I told her I'll never be jealous of Landau Christ every girl should be so lucky but if we'd gone to Washington she wouldn't be back for two more days he didn't expect any help why'd she run out I was finished that was It.

I called her, she didn't say I'll be right over Joe I miss you but something cold like how are you I slammed down the phone slouched home in misery waited for her to come I had nothing to do with telephones corruption the decadence and destruction of face-to-face America where people had really talked, therefore she couldn't call sent a special delivery telling how much she loved I sounded so upset she afraid to return till I wanted her I didn't receive it for two days by which I piled up forty-eight hours, a little sleep substracted, of insanely perfect character destruction after I'd received the letter I couldn't believe it Joe Madison in one brief year fucked-up on Rufus—Iran, Fran, Lucy, three of best things/people to ever hit his life and that after years of preparing for just such a year and quick on feet something radically radically wrong something wrong something a lie way down to the bottom of all I thought I wanted, something inside a killer, killing off all this at fruition moments, maybe—it couldn't be—maybe I didn't want anything of what I had labored for, politics, power, romantic love, science of mice and men.

30

He was only slightly shorter than I, about five eleven or six feet tall, slim hipped, erect, blue jeaned and tennis shoed, windbreaker jacket, hair cut close, chocolate skinned, beautiful, and our eyes seemed to disappear in each other I went straight out into his eyes, I had tired of reading and swung out on one of my wide circle Village walks down Thompson Street to Washington Square around the fountain peering at all interesting faces or scenes or up at that comparatively wildest expanse of sky or back at Judson Hall's bell tower Italianate below moon or clouds back up glitter gulch MacDougal's swag and potpourri pouring cash into the bearded tills while Italians built murderous furies toward the invaders of THEIR neighbourhood voted for Tammany machine and clean morals who'd clean out the freelovers queers Negroes guitars commercialism on down quieter red-bricked Bedford always a quick look in at Cholmely's then across grey sooty traffic to Hudson to the White Horse where bought a beer back Perry Street to see if Alice home and talk few minutes of theatre and old times this night she wasn't and I'd started on Eleventh Street toward Seventh when I saw him.

I stopped pure reflex and our gaze continued than I strode on, why tired of goddam girls' emotions never find more beautiful guy than that how Homo universale without knowing haven't you dreamt and thought occasionally for years now Joe no thinking don't ruin it.

I turned and hurried back around the corner he still stood erect and slim. "Hi," I said.

"Hi."

We looked at each knowing and we smiled.

"I'm waiting for a friend here but I don't think he's coming."

"I've got a place, I mean I don't a friend of mine who's out of town loaned it to me a week," avoid all future consequences make this pure moment pure experiment no entangling fears, "you could come over for a while. It's cold out here."

"Sounds good man."

We fell into step walking silently through streets that usually I liked but now seemed boring I wanted to race him home. Adventure, new, to hell with all routine voyage voyage. I looked him over admiring his firm neck and he gazed at me in return.

At the apartment I felt embarrassed I could offer wine but didn't make coffee tea I didn't smoke actually a goddam poor host but I hated hosting or anything formal except I loved being at a good host's place maybe he did took is this what a girl thinks about how she can please never felt this way with a girl I did keep instant coffee I always said to girls you want to make a cup but with him it seemed presumptuous.

"All I have's instant coffee. Want a cup?"

"Sure, man. Cigarette?" He shook out two above the pack's edge precisely gestured proffered them.

"No, thanks."

"Nice pad you have here."

"Good of my buddy to lend it, yeah, he's got some bread." Come off it Madison why the broke workingclass routine I hate the bourgeois I want real aristocrats why should I be tarred that which I can't stand who else can then why live this way go to Lower East Side quit your job maybe I will—

He was from Jamaica, quiet-voiced, polite, in his early twenties, unemployed, lived in The Bronx but had Village friends if he had more money he'd live in the Village. The finished cups of coffee sat between us. He stashed his cigarette and looked at me. "Bedroom's in there?"

"Yeah, want a look?" At last past the critical point something would happen in there why couldn't I just out and say let's go to bed together it was obvious but always sweated through my shrinking delicacy Rufus, Fran, Lucy, how I hated to talk of the intimate, what really mattered, Bill could set me off on philosophy Jeanine and I never explored she probably thought it hopeless not ever expected it maybe, the others fought it out with me you're not very giving of yourself Bill told me a month previous what do you mean I said totally absolutely bewildered I talk to you about everything well almost he replied but how long have we known each other I notice with people you just meet you hardly ever give them anything look, I said, everybody likes Joe Madison I smile and act quite agreeable yeah but where's the real you you hate to give out with it I'm not criticizing at all he said in his most scientific tone of voice like describing his newest reaction temperature and time, everybody has to protect themselves and you do a real good job whaddya mean protect myself I open myself up to the world take in anything everything we both had to laugh I bitterly because even for me but I still really said only to myself even for me that can't be true alright Bill goddam who doesn't need a few defenses but why I defended against his small remark?

We turned to each other in the room dark except for some light from the front room lamp and put our arms around no breasts no soft his day old stubble against my cheek.

"I never done this before," I said sitting down on the bed's edge.

He sat down beside and silence spread.

"You don't have to go ahead. You want to stop? I understand." This man no advantages of life save youth and beauty so gentle with a stranger why could I not have been at least as good with Lucy or with Fran, had I ever with her virginity said I understand to reluctance I guess I had but I didn't really mean and this man sounded as if he did.

"No. I want to," I said, but I'm not going to be able to help you much I mean I do really want to but I just don't know how to I can't let myself go."

We slowly took off our clothes. "You're beautiful," I said.

"You're not bad, man, now relax. You sure you want to?"

"Yes!" don't talk anymore let's go ahead let's go ahead.

I lay there stiff and boardlike while he labored with devotion skill mastery Lucy you responded at least once a night why did it seem to me so intolerable you couldn't always roll and go why am I locked within, my pelvic region fell away from my stiff back and unyielding mind it swayed and moved a thing apart though later its relaxation flowed upward he finished my lower body finished he rose to go to the bathroom and water ran should kiss him but I can't we dressed "You were very good," I said how often some girl had said that to me did they mean no more I always left exalted proud proved-out thinking I'd really communicated really left them with something besides a worry till their next period proved it groundless and a momentary relaxation "I'm sorry I didn't please you more," he said perceptive bastard "You did," I said "really you were very good," and really he had been, Christ if Lucy had those techniques and lavished them so tenderly I'd follow her to China I had no guilt feelings anxieties Michelangelo and Plato why hadn't I really sung what a cold fish.

He smoked another cigarette. "Well, thanks, man," he said very polite.

"Thank *you*," I said and saw him to the door hope he believes this place's not really mine but whether that or discouraged or contemptuous he never returned I actually made myself alone first time ever a pot of hot water poured it in a cup added two teaspoonfuls of instant one of sugar stirred drank it and then another.

31

Iran not the only land with lost empires and dreams. Lester Mellon and I drove up the abandoned Lincoln Continental Highway they'd called it bouncing down the two ruts over fifty years old didn't rain a lot in that part of Wyoming but gullies still cutting into sagebrush right up into the mountains we headed for, a cattle empire already overgrazed and lost in 1890, mainly sheep now, antelope bounded over a rise and disappeared all but the old male he turned at the very top and looked back checking us out we figured before rejoining the group, as we drove off that old main road we hit a ranch trail but the sodbusters that followed the cattlemen their old shacks deserted too, of course Indian arrowheads probably around maybe Folsom points, no place on earth but's old enough to be steeped in disappearance, a wildcat bobtailed sunofagun almost big as a mountain lion jumped down on the sandy road about a hundred feet in front of us slunk three steps across and disappeared in the buckbrush probably hot after one or both the two fawns we'd just seen. Pulling with everything the pickup had down in low we climbed up out of the last vee of the valley and toward the high ledges look Lester said his finger on the map his eyes alert that's old Silver City, a few roofless crumbling stone houses a little graveyard just before us, it must have been because fenceposts and here and there dangling rusted wire wild roses it was late June all over, quite a boomtown once over ten thousand people, yellow mounds bloomed over the mountainside where each man had gophered, the bed of the old narrowgauge railway still stuck up like a levee except where gullies had eaten through don't crucify us on a cross of gold rallies and the Silver Bloc they tried to save themselves a ratio of gold/silver prices cureall for America now silver in the space/electronic age worth something else than money, actual practical or at any rate industrial future in silver and even its lead/zinc buddies all there in those veins of quartz splayed through the mountain core by millions year old explosions of the hot compressed under this cold wrinkling up and down crust, terra firma what a laugh but for an animal shortlived as man comparativey so even though Grecian cities already sunk beneath the sea Pompeii beneath the lava at any rate it could be mined again for less money than the product could be sold for if indeed the reserves extended down from the gopher holes, they did that way my conviction and if Lester and I could prove it or convince Rufus and certain financiers roadbuilders smelterbuilders and all the rest including appropriate government agencies then all would move again right here at home and Madison you might still make it only craftier subtler from all your life lessons to governor and president.

I knew them all Washington Adams Jefferson we're all Federalists and Republicans end of the old aristocracy's rule Munroe Jackson cheated by the narrow minded NewEnglander New England revisionists call outstanding because he served in the House of Representatives at life's end Jackson finally made it, at New Orleans I looked down on the battle field from top of huge aluminum plant tower, the British hadn't been so stupid Old Hickory had water to his rear left and right and if the British had made it over the cotton bales we might not have gotten Florida anyway Little Van a used-up man and all that hopeless procession except for Polk who annexed the West passed all his legislation retired after one term inexplicable to me, who more successful? why did he quit? Polk perhaps America's one real refutation of life-consuming ambition.

Lincoln whom Herndon compared to Caeser in his ambition and cold shrewdness, poor old Grant, if Teddy hadn't roughshod in on anarchist assassination and a Socialist President or at least powerful party would have emerged, World History and Wilson the Kennedy hoping brilliant looking for his chance finally shot down, his shooter shot and nothing else happened it all moved on I mean why did I want it I did I didn't, but ambition runs uphill and shining there Washington Jefferson Lincoln and I have declared eternal hostility upon this continent tyranny over the human mind to decide upon this continent whether fear itself or government deriving just powers from consent of governed of by and for the people pursuing life liberty and happiness shall or shall not perish from the earth and everybody studying by candlelight in rain-leaking log cabins shall enrapture the working farmers and they dropping plows shall gather round Athenians are possible on the plains but they're depopulated and we burrow down in Harlem and suburbia nonetheless oh if I could tell brothers sisters what's in my heart you should weep such tears I tell you America is blessed you know it I know it everyone knows it because we took the open road and we found this place some of us dreamed dreams so great no society will ever overtake and pass them why can't we love and rollick share and share our great good fortune that's why I want to be president I want to labor on this cause—

Lester and I advanced to the portal, a small rock slide had left only a foot and a half entrance to the main mine which certain capitalists devised to work efficiently all the smaller holdings they'd bought. We put on hard hats finally and taking flashlight in hand moved down the drift farther and farther into dark why the hell risking life on this but far enough along hard to turn back though deep down water trickled/glistened and our boots grew soggy and piles of rock lay between the foursquare beams.

After a week we were convinced. Driving over Coyote flats unshaven gloating we congratulated ourselves, "Goddam it, Lester, there's two million pounds down there, recoverable, that's thirty-five million plus the lead and zinc, and there must be ten or more sites like this, we've proved it out, we're going to ride, man!"

"Call it Rufus Brown number one," he said grinning. "Your company really knows how to turn a good man loose."

Only one decrepit green phone booth in Beryl, outside the one cafe, good steaks though and always a second cup of coffee, they had a special breakfast for "he-men", steak, ten eggs, bacon, peaches, biscuits, gravy, coffee, claimed actually a couple of guys had ordered and eaten in the last decade, I dialed the operator, "Manhattan," I said, "where's that?" "New York City Area Code 212–"

Rufus had died the night before. Slumped down dead. The company would carry on. Finish it up, Joe. The Company. A cold word. I'd worked for companies before. I hated companies. Rufus Brown I worked for–he could see right through me, call me to account, often wrong, but he talked things right through, he tried for the big things, he remained among the chronium glitter of Success my last link with American history when I talked with him I felt him still a plain man, plain, how can a man ever be plain, he glowed and cried to think how his shined shoes his spiffy suit and tie so irritated me, because he hadn't needed them, alone of all men I knew, he could've stood in a toga, draped a white sheet, cranky, seen all the failures, disillusioned, knowing how frail he and others yet that something happens, "Get the relevant data, survey possibilities, dreams, make your programs large, Joe, but advance step by step testing all the time. Realize what happens will be yours, part of the dream will survive, it will have endured reality and not all of it will be found wanting and be cast aside, you will find out what survives."

My grandfather, I'd thrown a cat into the mudpuddle, five-year-old laughing at its mewling and spluttering, did you throw the cat in, yes, turn around, I did and he kicked me hard face first into the mudpuddle, that's how the cat felt. Bob Henreid my first big industrial job I'd said I know this is right Bob it'll make better titanium than ever before but it's a hundred thousand dollar risk on the titanium alone not counting all the side effects morale and what not these were the rush days of fifty-seven, had to get the strength/weight ratios up for Jets and Rockets, he said big broad shouldered you have it worked out don't you yessir then think of it just like carbon steel science and engineering don't change principles with money cost, do you think it'll work yes go ahead unless you don't have any faith in yourself, Prof Samuels harsh voiced perfect articulation acidulous do you think Madison this passage is fine literature from old testament about a hundred thousand dead corpses yessir very definitely oh he said looking around at the class Madison thinks tautologies make fine literature my father beating me down again and again showing me how to break through the toughest line giving me all his lore use your hands, use your feet, drive, your knees, drive, your shoulders, drive, your head, drive, come on, hit me hard, drive, drive, use everything you've got.

I love you fathers all I sit here leaned forward in my chair writing on the blanket machined rectilinear imitation of ancient flowing Berber style and goddam it Rufus I know this is full of stylistic incongruities I'm remembering who I pushed in mud-puddles and shit I'm handling my soul as freely as I would carbon steel reverencing and infuriated with both such strength such rusting I'm forgetting all cliches about fine literature I'm trying to live this word by word I'm using my hands, my feet, they're chilled in my boots in January even Marrakesh is cold there's no rugs on their floors, no heat, my head, my heart, my guts, my cock, my belly, my asshole, I'm using everything I've got, I know none of you can help hurt me anymore you made it tough you taught me I picked up a little of it I too have eternal hostility for all chains and I'm writing for people to read, it's by me a people and I'm certainly of so many people even as I do this wonder if any of you would approve or understand how much this all from you but whether or not I come forward producing this and take now at least in my own mind/feelings my place with you fathers Rufus father even you tribal presidents all of us brothers we do what we can with this unleashed dream, America maddens us with unattainable truth exaltation and splendor and all of us survey the ruins that we have garnered, and Lincoln's second inaugural, threnody of guilt foreboding plays the secret music of our hearts, what might he have said had he foreseen the further Indian slaughters, the massed and huddled peasantry yearning in the Cities, world annihilation threats, the damp wadding stuffed into our minds, the prohibitions innumerable and nasty.

32

Ruins. Outside of reading and museum walking therefore second hand I'd known only one artist I don't mean people doing what's the current phrase workmanlike competent dreaming or word stringing together or talented girls but an artist who produced produced dreamed struggled with technique flamed of all places I met him in Columbus, Ohio, seven years before my God it's like yesterday now the big aqueducts crumbling and only the genuine springs flow on natural drainage I had a two months research job a special cobalt extraction pilot plant and really bored always searching for new things I went to a local writer's group this woman about twenty-nine, looked at me intensely during the meeting and afterwards insisted on talking though I tried to escape because she draped an off shoulder black gown with sequin glints short hairdo and that before their popularity and still somehow she projected dowdy and all pent-up.

You must meet my husband.

Oh

You must meet him you and he are meant to meet

Just how do you think you hardly know me

He's a sculptor/artist you'd love his things

Probably I'm sure if he's like the writing group God save me

I'm sure you would that's just it he's not at all

Allright

When don't just say it I really mean it how about tomorrow night

Allright allright

I hate being pushed the woman had the fanatic gleam probably brainwashed by some slob who couldn't make it playing God out here in the corn country

She called my landlady next afternoon at six and asked for me

Are you coming at eight

Of course I'll be over

I'd been planning to skip out had just found the local pickup bar and the girl next door who undressed parading behind gauze curtain only fifteen air feet away about two hundred fifty walking feet away daughter of next door therefore complicated psychic miles away maybe even in another dimension altogether had me very hot she'd put on quite a show last night never looked in my direction though did leave my window open fair play and all that besides something might eventually happen mostly of course I read reaction kinetics I wished I'd gone to the mountains but when the blackgowned off-shoulder fanatic her shoulder's were extraordinarily clear skinned although bony she thin all over Shaughnessy said I work only from experience that is primal fingertip sensations however imaginatively recombine that's why my women shallowchested he grinned gleaming toothed his lower lip wet he stared with penetrating disorchestration at you head close as a Latin American's when he really interested anyway when she called to check up even I maverick pure mongreled orneriness had to say really meaning it now "of course".

We'd never lost touch before I left for Tangiers only talked every six months or so but always Shaughnessy in my mind's background I always like to know men of many origins and kinds but he and I had a special closeness besides his being unique among my friends we could talk of anything and go deep.

Jim I'm thinking of throwing over everything

We walked along Brooklyn Heights promenade admiring bay's splendor look he'd said I love Manhattan this view of it most fantastic growth I've ever seen Growth natural/cancerous not built Shaughnessy's words often resonated through me as if special meanings roiled within we sat down on a bench.

Everything that's a lot, you committing suicide?

I mean quitting Worldwide quitting that whole world of not working for any company ever again except just for bread to eat sleep dress travel some

If you do quit you ought to quit all the way but it seems to me you're doing very well now if you're going to come back to that world.

I know nobody's going to be better than Worldwide they're all sharp subtle know the score efficient liberal but I mean I can't take it any longer

You talked a little like this in '56 in Columbus. I quit that place came here but you went on I thought you'd made up your mind to be president or secretary of state or something

Oh that's all a joke I don't want to anymore I can't anyway you know something I even picked up a beautiful guy on the street the other day

What

Yeah I said to hell with it there's only one life I want to live it I mean really personally actually beyond personally the persona mask all a construct and can't find any unity or goal inside either I built imaginary architectonics but the structures all collapsed like Worldwide's giving me a chance on big international project essential to an advancing future in America but I can't take being A Company Man, the rich the intelligent the well-connected the sexy Fran wanted to give me a lifetime contract I refused to sign, and Bill's lab if I became a salesman might make us the legendary millions what in the fuck Jim's it all for

Tell me more about the guy you picked up

He was slim erect chocolate skinned and so damned decent

Was he any good did he know how to use his tongue

He was allright very good yes

Did you like it

I couldn't hardly relax I was pretty stiff a scared virgin

You should've let me taken your cherry I'm wild in bed

I laughed

I mean it I would've loved to break you in I never thought you would

It's different with you you're my friend

What's a friend for you take a chance on pickups you don't know what you're letting yourself in for some guys are nuts about this kind of thing you know.

But I want to talk with you about quitting

You're talking too big too general what do you want to do Are you doing to quit girls

No

You going to try girls and boys both

No I dont think so maybe

You want to be fucked in the ass at all

I think about it sometimes damn you're really putting it to me

You going to loaf and travel

Maybe I'll write about it all

You don't write just by quitting your job if that's what you really want to do you write because you want to write

I want to write

You'll never be president or anything like that if you really write those people out there won't like it besides if you anywhere even way deep down want coming back it'll show it'll hang you up you'll only be trading in a good man of action for a lousy writer

I don't think it's left anywhere

Would you publish under your own name

Yes I think so

Will you

Yes I will knowing that I lied

Where will you go

I don't know around the world

If you write it's coming from you why don't you live in Hoboken that's the place someplace like that cheap comparatively around New York you don't have to set out on a run unless you're worried it's coming after you

Maybe it will Christ Jim I'm trying I don't want to take chances I want to go all out I want to make a break like I want to split

Is the most important thing really writing it isn't is it

No I want to live Jim I want to do what when where how I please or at least meet the No's outside me not inside. I want to understand even if that leads to understanding there's no understanding I want time to talk to people hours or days at a time if something to say to each other I want to see strange customs help build a few wilder stranger ones I feel like I've been pushed all my life I made high grades played football worked even when I quit school and bummed around the country I always worked I mean at hard physical jobs I don't resent it I loved it at the time it built me a good body I appreciate why do I protest so I studied faithfully economics science philosophy politics literature I tried always to make more money for a company than they paid me I even watched precincts God Jim I started to cry I even watched precincts in Chicago the ones were giving the other chicken dinner and hauling drunks in literally by the overcoat collar to vote going inside the booth with them I protested and called a cop Jim I thought God knows what working for democracy freedom future knowledge so I could use power to really transform it sounds like a joke to me now Jim it's funny now but I did all those things and it was torture let me tell you that Jim I don't want marriage settling down home children car telephone television seems to me now such horror I could I believe actually flee if somebody tried to hand it to me in a golden sunset my life's into pieces Jim same as yours back in '56 my nights are totally different from days my weekends another universe I'm collapsing into moments like beads with the string jerked out I called this being Homo universale I opened myself to rape from all objects and people the great yea-sayer no more Jim I say No now I can really at last say some No's some Yes's too but I'm going to start with a great big NO I don't want it anymore and I start out with dread not fear because I've lived with fear fear of being discovered fear of losing anything I make that's real by some pretenders maybe the pretenders are the ones that have to hit you all the harder because you're what they might become if only they dared. I'd worked so hard I actually made myself finish a whole semester drawing rectilinear shit with T-squares I used to be sick with madness fantasy throwing my drawing board out the window take it Joe take it Joe I'd say remember your great goals it's part of the game millions have done it so can you the same thing dragged us through basic training crawling under the barbed wire though I'm artistic/basic enough I liked that a hell of a lot better than drawing stupid square lines when I knew I'd never be a draughtsman but only have them working for me and Jim I actually got soft with myself and said you poor shit relax forget about an A take a B, but dread I mean of finding nothing, that there isn't anything better more lively that all any twigged hairy doomed human has besides his drawing board jobs is nothing that we're just sugar cubes dropped into a great pot of whirling nothing and we just dissolve away but I don't care anymore Jim I've ended pushing I'm going to—I don't know—something very different.

When was it two years before I'd written him from Harvard I'm sick of it I have to talk to you he'd written fine and I on a bitterly windcold December day hiked from the Greyhound bus on Fiftieth to his apartment on West Forty-Seventh long concrete grey halls down to the tiny dark toilet in back sewing the four apartments two in each side up to the fifth floor a soupy shitting poverty smell pervading and it hit me hard fresh from redbrick ivy freshly daily made crisp bed big desk bookcase hot showers across the hall large clean dining halls could I really give it up Vincent Sheehan ended his between the war's odyssey happy in British bourgeois old Penelope, it's no joke to be cold and dirty flearidden and I had no income, when I was a kid nothing bothered you soft bastard what's wrong with you now Hi Jim I said

Look excited he dragged out his latest things better than ever I'll have a show in another year or two

He left Columbus two weeks after I did that summer of '56 he said you want to come back to the garage his studio a minute

Sure I loved to watch him work touch and examine his tools and materials

I'm smashing it all he said

Come on I laughed sure we had quite a talk last week you're going to New York but smash it all

All

You need the money Christ at least look it'll set you up for a year to do what you want

He raised up a bull that would've sold anywhere between the Hudson River and San Francisco bay as high art.

Don't smash that let me buy it my God

I don't want any of this around with the name of Shaughnessy

Save that bull at least there's something to it

Not enough he slow deliberate poise and hurled it on the concrete perfectly red brown glazed baked clay burst spread out in many almost flat pieces ten works in all disappeared

It'll take me five or six years but I'll make new ones enough for several shows

I made a special trip to the Village from Pittsburgh to see him he lived in four by seven alcove off a large goodlooking homo sexual's pad whom he did designs for, also four hours a day for a display company he looked thin we walked for hours

When I first came here he said I had nothing Molly took it all I walked around as if I were dead I said Shaughnessy there's no faking it you must die I walked across streets without looking for cars I nearly froze I had only slacks a shirt a thin jacket somebody gave me this belted raincoat then this job I decided I had to learn to live all over again how to eat to walk talk with people sex I went wild as an infant tried anything of course that lets women out they're too conventional frightened complicated you want to hear some stories

Yes you writing too now

No these only in my mind I'll never write them down they keep me from going mad an old lady grey spinster takes a young boy to the choirmaster break him in right she says was there ever such a woman the young boy when the choirmaster finishes runs back to the old lady you did me such a favor now I'll break you in right it's still not too late was there ever such a boy and the old lady and choirmaster lived happily forever after but the boy had to grow up and learn again what he forgot by that time so old he didn't really care but one day he mumbled his secret to a small boy who reminded him of himself because a hot summer day shivered him with a sudden smell and the small boy wound up in jail and hates the old man who's now dead

He showed me a good lowcost restaurant on Fourth Street don't let it upset you he said the waiters'll go for you. That's the only luxury I ask for from life, a place to work and sleep I don't call a luxury, a good place to eat out. Shaughnessy couldn't help being elegant one time he'd almost taken a Swedenborgian ministry I bet he really turned on the old furry dowagers.

33

I wanted to shatter Lucy I see now that I'm shattered myself this morning the African dancer at Djenema el Fna the patriarch white turbaned red burnoosed and glasses advanced to me look I thought already contributed my ten francs two cents that's my daily quota he knows that maybe thinks for every day it's too little he pulled my arm he suddenly just risen from crosslegged position watching the five boys two young men dance one boy beating a drum with the hooked Saharan sticks he did the special rhythms a young man beat the other provided the steady unaccented background hey okay yeah I'll dance sprung up and down around twisted to fill in the gaps where hadn't learned their steps quite when my muscles turned watery I'd responded directly to his touch no hesitation almost none and then sitting in my new hotel room deeper in the Medina one window open to courtyard the other across the street to a blue stone alternating with brown adobe house wall clean air from last night's rain warm when you wear a sweater and sportcoat I looked up across the courtyard to the higher adjoining wall a Berber girl young waved to me we figured out a way I climbed over her wall the rooftops belong to women here but still the men supposed to be very against westerners with their women it made an extra thrill she was sorting the last chaff from what grains spread out on an old multicolored cloth we both knew a few French words that's all we squatted and I helped her pick out a little chaff she uncomfortable at my doing woman's work agreed to meet at eight dark that's what I really wanted, to shatter Lucy where she flowed out from under to meet just simply me flowing no hesitations no language there must have been a way—

We'd tried one last time that winter early March she'd returned from Florida freshly re-suntanned we both agreed very slowly we have bad memories pain, went to Frick gallery she an hour late I angry we hiked through Central Park looked at glacial striations relaxed soaked in the view almost the whole place to ourselves though it wasn't that cold and then dinner together a couple of nights tried slowly talking over things and subject she took me up to see two children in Harlem she was especially interested in we'd just about felt ready to go again planned a dinner and whole evening together I had my brainstorm invite Bill and we could discuss anything Bill would moderate our tempers.

You aren't really interested in arguing politics she shouted

Discussing

Argue discuss who cares it's something else between us why you keep on

I'm only trying to explain to you what socialism is

I know what it is how can a capitalist tell me what it is

You've got a yearning for the primitive commune composed of depth analyzed sophisticated individuals confused with socialism which is an economic system not psychology/anthropology and I'm former left-wing union organizer.

Look Bill broke in maybe it's just a question of semantics

It's not semantics she shouted he's not admitting what makes him argue

Learn to discuss one subject at a time and do it thoroughly I shouted that's the trouble with you half-ass educated girls you read one book you hear one guy like Landau talk and you think you are an authority

I don't just quote Landau

Yeah you don't you misquote him

We had to leave the Hip Bagel I cringed we'd been shouting

so loud the manager asked us to cool it

Outside I shut up this was it then we'd never had anything in common except my projected dream upon a subway image and a moment of stormy affection in the Kiwi two lonely people in the Big City Romance we'd thought we had it what a weary trivial story let Bill and her talk I'm finished it's hopeless why can't they relax

We continued walking to the deserted mailbox lobby of my building I lounged against the door deliberately not opening it something terrible inside how would it express itself

Let me give you another example Bill said one time I was talking about vanadium reactions and I used the word

Oh Christ I thought Lucy stood hair disarrayed back against one tier of mail boxes Bill his back to the other I observed them both coldly maliciously, I ought to say goodbye to Bill, Lucy and I'd then go upstairs I truly believe we'd embrace each other we both see it's not politics we're arguing about we want to hold each other and somehow we're not going to it's all going to be destroyed unless I stop this scene I knew I wouldn't I'm going to make a telephone call I said and dialed another girl for a date the next night, returning they still doggedly discussing words well goodnight I said elaborately casual I think I'll get some sleep hope you two can work it out hell let her make a one night stand with Bill maybe it'll help him loosen up she turned a look toward me I wished I'd never seen but I didn't waver, so long I clicked the door locked behind me and left them in that yellow light between the mailbox tiers in the glassed narrow modern lobby when I undressed and lay in bed I felt dirty as vomit

And yet that next summer I'd met her and Sally in the West we'd had two good days in the mountains the first night she'd slept between us all of us in sleeping bags she afraid of what might snuffle/shuffle in the night the river bubbled behind us in the morning she washed her face and combed her long hair take a picture of me please she'd bought the fanciest equipment I crawled on the gravel Sally laughing a straddle a fallen cottonwood behind us until I framed that face so evanescent snub pert then passionate relaxed female then suntanned model beauty then forlorn poor rich girl behind society mask then wrinkling nose in disdain then fiery no-nonsense attacking all oppression of the week click if I caught only part of her that'd be a good one

After Durango I decided again all hopeless but might as well go on I wanted to see the country too after all she and Sally good people important in my life I should show them the Navajo and canyon country

Lucy woke up at nine oh we were going to leave early we slept late we must go see Sally maybe she's lonely but Sally snoozed on dead to the world Lucy tickled one set of ribs I the other Sally sat up and kissed first one of us then the other is it really time to leave excited

Yes yes many things to see

34

At least once a day on that trip through the Indian/ canyon country I'd say Lucy damn it I took this week off to see my folks I've made up my mind and I really had except for backsliding doubts once a week at least that I'm chucking it all what a lot of phrases we've built up in the old language for that act taking off heading out splitting to hell with it so long Charlie I've had it off into the wild blue hit the rails fed up or to the gills greener pastures leaving for the wide open spring me on the lam taking a powder making a break for it that lovely imperishable always gleaming in gloaming besprayed transient every changing/luring color whatever it is it's not boondocks is worth a clutch of sparrows in the hand and that's why I leave meadowlarks in the boondocks but also hie myself there anyhow she'd say what a lovely trip I'm feeling better each day your holding me at night helps we'd started unzipping the top half of our sleeping bags and I slipped my hands under blouse sweater and bra to hold her all night through in the mornings I'd watch the sun rise she and Sally sleeping so peacefully clear complexioned almost translucent I never could wake them it seemed too brutal though they always said we want to see the sunrise they were catching up on sleep sleep sleep and fresh air they'd missed in hectic city months or wild resort places or working on the Washington Civil Rights march everyday they more radiant somehow I couldn't leave them we finally arrived at San Francisco Lucy's extraordinary apartment she'd flown out the month before and found bay overlooking and I chucked I suppose practically all Lucy and I'd built up on the trip down the drain in a fit of remorse at only one day left to see my folks the last maybe because my grandmother/mother both ill very efficient I demanded plane reservations called folks said I'll be in Dallas tomorrow pm can you pick me up they had to drive hundred and fifty miles but I could make two hours because of non-stop flight over the airport sixty miles from where they lived in Indian State now every minute seemed precious and that night I refused to sleep with Lucy and Sally very irritable I told her how much do you think a man can stand she stood hesitant in the doorway you really should she said to hell with it I said and rolled over as if exhausted if I'd gone to her I'd never left her on the morrow I had to break away make a scene the next morning she'd been going to show us the Berkeley campus I got up at six in vindictive high spirits I dressed took off without leaving a note caught a bus saw the campus myself returned to find Lucy alone businesslike doing property things Sally had left too Lucy'd had to wait for me I thought you wanted to sleep late I said I left at six no I was eager to show you things today I woke at seven I know you have to leave this afternoon suddenly I could've sat down and cried but I knew it was no use someday maybe you and I will really make it I said it's hard for me to trust you after last winter she said maybe so but after I finish up my formal studies I'm twenty-three now I guess I've learned enough the books won't be just a hindrance then I can distinguish what's for real you'll do it I said I believe you'll really do it you have everything money brains looks youth a heart you will too she said I laughed yeah sure the day fell apart into waiting for Sally's return driving through traffic for lunch driving through traffic to show me some places especially significant to her I tense miserable at leaving said yeah driving through traffic to the airport it all seemed so hopeless we'd gotten in another big political argument she leaned across the front seat a kiss didn't seem worthwhile I shook her hand well maybe I'll come back from Africa/Asia via the Golden Gate let me know in advance she said goodbye goodbye

Sure enough my father stood a big man grey haired now an inch taller than myself light reflecting from his rimless glasses that pinched two deep red spots on each side of his nose from the metal holders he wouldn't get plastic ones my mother small so small she now down to ninety pounds her glasses hung by long necklace down across her blouse well traveler my father said we shook hands, the first time I'd actually left home and worked fourteen arriving back on the bus from California he and mother waiting backs against the redbrick wall we'd shaken hands he'd given me a funny look and planted a cold wet kiss on my lips I glanced embarrassed to see if anyone looking it was kind of nice but I resented it hadn't I been a man for three months earning my own way my mother and I always just brushed lips we never really kissed.

Joe she said unless you're hungry why don't we just jump in the car your grandmother really wants to see you

I want to see her

We can get there just before she goes to sleep I brought some fruit and chocolate chip cookies you can nibble on those

Fine

I would have made your special cake but I didn't have time you just called last night

I know don't worry

My father drove with a practiced hand seventy miles an hour he'd been raised in a sod dugout trapped otter and mink and he handled every machine like he'd owned it a lifetime I wish he'd shown me how to trap when I was very young and he coached football out in the Western part of the state shortgrass country we called it part of the dust bowl in USA lingo and of course back then the sun did set sometimes at two in the afternoon in a red-cloud obliterating west he'd taken me one time another man with him and we'd lain very quiet out in the prairie slightly chill gradually blades of grass appeared, between them grey earth the blades were kind of far apart look he'd said Where Way down there a long ways off some spots they appeared/ disappeared Prairie dogs popping in and out of their holes he and the other man got very intense paid no more attention to me brought the wooden part of their rifles to their right shoulders their left hand snaked out along the metal part my ears ached with the noise an acrid smell pinched my nose

They're all down in their holes now my father said quietly

We walked over the long prairie millions of grassblades everything was light and grey now except a yellow round sun that had just lost all its red becoming smaller every time I looked I struggled to keep up with four huge legs booted and thick ridged pants they were powerful up and down up and down he picked me up want some help put me down put down finally there they picked up four balls of fur I didn't see before at the edge of all the little mounds of dirt

This is a prairie dog city they live with rattlesnakes and owls now there are no more prairie dog cities in the short grass country they broke horse's legs when you galloped through them and you had to shoot the horses that's why it was allright to shoot prairie dogs besides you couldn't shoot very many because prairie dogs were very alert and you had to sneak up on them like an Indian and then you had to shoot real fast because they dived for their holes and didn't come back for a long time beavers I later found out in the Rockies and the White Mountains the same way only just seeing them they dived under Bill Layton and I always liked to look for beavers not just the dams channels and houses but real live beavers in action anyway four prairie dogs was a good haul but they did scientific research economic analysis a kind of Iran project I guess in its small way and prairie dogs disappeared I looked at one with real interest at the Central Park Zoo at New York City with Lucy when we were walking from Frick Gallery maybe that's what helped me get over my mad at her being late I told her some of this story and the little protected rodent chomped away on I believe it was actually a carrot.

35

From whatever trip I'd ever taken I always tried to stop by to see my grandmother, she was now eighty-seven they'd thought she wouldn't live much longer but mother said she'll probably outlive us all one boy killed in World War II one daughter died six left but my mother and her oldest brother ill two of her grandsons dead she had I'd lost count twenty or twenty-one great grandchildren maybe that was three years ago maybe now thirty I hadn't seen some cousins for years we all· used to gather every Christmas at grandfather's huge lightning-rod adorned house sitting smackdab in the middle of the road that went straight to town only of course it didn't the road had to stop and turn into a T in front of granddad's house and that's why the road ended I always figured Granddad wanted to stand on the front porch and look straight ahead a mile into Main Street he had a big painting of a racehorse but he'd died before I came along betting and gambling were considered kind of evil but I knew granddad really loved racing he used to take me out to the country he was sixty-six, seven, eight and I sixty years younger he'd tell me stand up back of the front seat and he'd turn the old Ford loose eighty miles an hour down the country road all you could see out the backwindow dust Yee-haw he'd laugh and I'd scream/yell in pleasure/fright your grandmother's very ill my father said earnestly

You always say that but when I see her she's always perky

Well you don't come by often anymore maybe once a year she's been pretty sick let me tell you

He turned the car on to the gravel drive granddad's old smokehouse gone hams bacons onions potatoes his goldfish ponds filled with prairie dust and lawned over one time he'd tried a goat to keep the lawn down but it did an uneven job the hog wallows long filled the last ruins of the old bran mill filled the chickenhouse gone the old barn grey shrunken planks you could see through my uncle killed on the submarine he'd used to be a rodeo hand joined the navy to see the world didn't see none of it he said the skipper wouldn't let any of us look through the periscope we were right in Tokyo bay he said sorry I can't let any of you see the world they're coming at us with depth charges that was '42 they'd gone right in the Bay and sunk ships he was a hero and had a decoration they'd finally set him to teaching others in Massachusetts or some outlandish place and he'd gotten tired of fooling around volunteered for another duty tour and disappeared that uncle twenty years younger than my mother everybody loved him because he was right in between us nephews and nieces and the aunts uncles actually he and one cousin of mine always argued who was older that uncle used to nail sheepskins on the barn door to dry now I like to touch the ones Moroccans try to sell me he was also the one who put catfish in the cattle tank to grow up

What the hell I'd worked all that out I ran up the red standstone flag path that was still there and into the kitchen my grandmother no longer slept upstairs but in the dining room next to the kitchen I never saw her quite so the only word I know's pure her hair completely white her skin so pale in past always sunburned even just leathery brown had turned pale and delicate like a little girl's Gran in that big castle couldn't have had more delicate skin her old smallpox pits even had almost worn away she'd had a few hairs on her upper lip a little bristly they lay so soft/white almost invisible her eyes somewhat tired but mischievous gleam as ever, she understood the world when I despaired of fathers mothers brothers girls friends I always knew grandmother understood never once had she ever criticized I stayed every summer with her if I wanted money I chopped weeds she always hid a cookie jar on the top pantry shelf we all knew where it was but it wouldn't have been any fun you had to sneak in the dark not fair to switch on the light silently put her stepladder over and take out pocketfulls of cookies it didn't even cost dessert because she always had chocolate cake or banana pie for dessert, anyway we ran it off by suppertime though sometimes I read without objection because probably no one knew what was in her eldest boy's left-behind glass windowed bookcase library old copies of the Nation Thorstein Veblen on the Leisure Class Das Kapital and seven candalabraed mystery of Madagascar that I read every summer hoping it would always frighten me but the fourth time when I was ten it didn't I was very disappointed

I caught her hands they soft now softer than a courtesan of France she'd had to have a woman do for her the last three years when she'd sat down for the first time a bad stroke hit her she'd told me ten years before they tell me to sit down and take it easy Joe I'll never sit down till I have a stroke because I see when old people sit down they never get up again. She'd taken up flying and long distance traveling she'd come to see me in Colorado studying and Washington farming and Florida in the army and Missouri in the army my folks had come too somehow a special joy Grandmother came she'd pull out her diabetes needle and jab it the loose skin of her upper arm the old flab can't feel nothing no more, leather I guess ee-ee she laughed grinning I bet she was a freckled tomboy back in the 1880's.

The old potbellied stove gone where we'd burnt wood and coal, gas heater now, she'd even had a woodburning cooking stove when I was a boy kerosene lamps out at my aunt's place down the road Roosevelt REA all electric now how many Rufus Brown's had labored heart/soul/mind but I liked the old way better you're a sentimental fool and the women worked their fingers to the bone but I did I do wouldn't you be glad to have a good electric lamp and warm gas stove in Marrakesh Medina yes but no not if it means all the rest not if it means an end to the quilting parties my grandmother and the neighbouring women sewed gorgeousness out of old scraps if Berber's art's destroyed if the Pueblos disappear in the City slums if all us Okies become California bourgeois fatbellied and wheeling down the traffic jammed horizon no I'm not sentimental it was better it wasn't so simple either every mining camp of ten thousand population had an opera house and Shaxpere then one had Mark Twain and another Ambrose Bierce and now all New York City puts on three plays in Central Park a year and Stamford Connecticut a couple and if I mistake me not no presidents beat Lincoln Jefferson or roughing it T.Roosevelt's for intellect but what the hell no culture's eternal lay the frontier that burned in fourteen generations' hearts to rest and old dream of yeoman fleeing the puritan moralizers the city lawyers tyrants capitalists all the put-downers, they wanted elbow room no wonder they all liked Shaxpere the bloody fifth and midsummer magic of beautiful women and was against the merrie Englande they even sent the Methodist circuit riders after us they encircled us with railroads they cut us to pieces with highways they drowned us in radio noise and TV pictures they luxuried us to death with Electricity and indoor toilets they Monkey Ward'd and Sears Roebuck'd us into fashion with their catalogues now metamorphosed to Vogue and Esquire and the young rebels read *Playboy* I danced with a syphilitic whore in Butte the Hill high with yellow ginger and mining gallows against the sky she thought she was the last Assiniboine her two brothers both killed in the mine rock blasts she laughed bitterly I bought her two beers I even drank two myself with her how count the Indian tribes gunned down the Black cultures wiped out the Jews ghettoed watch the Catholics just now moving to the hilltops of Pennsylvania out the sooty valleys but we we Anglo Saxons went down too, listen to me here at least Lucy you in full revolt about the crimes of your father WE went down too everybody has gone down and trembles in front of their TV set waiting for holocaust cheer cheer for freedom you can choose between dee and dum every four years and make ten thousand dollars every year.

My grandmother sat up my mother shouted in her ear

I can never make her hear my mother went in the kitchen to help the woman fix up food my grandmother always called it vittles I couldn't find it in the dictionary my father laughed and pointed to victuals like my grandfather roared belly and my mother said stomach and we cousins all liked to watch cow shit splashing down to form what would become a round hard turd they didn't smell at all out in the wind/sun/rain one would sail quite a ways when you tossed it and it grew a big problem what to call it finally

My Grandmother started telling me about her farm I guess the last time you were here I told you old man Jones had just about sold me his half well I thought I could get him down to six thousand but I couldn't so now he won't sell I guess I outsmarted myself ee-ee her high laugh ironical and meditative

You always came here didn't you no matter how far away

Yes

I went to see you too didn't I

Yes

Her soft fingers stroked the palm of my hand she'd felt so much flesh so many living people she was called Grandma Brand by everyone in town except of course the newcomers in their big ranch style houses along the highway who commuted every day into State City that's forty miles on a concrete line

You stayed a long time

Only tonight

Only tonight

Yes my mother said he flew in she raised her voice he flew in but it's important he get back to New York City

New York City

Yes Mama He's got an important conference in New York City

36

Bill we've got to have a peyote party again.
yeah but the stuff tastes so bad
didn't you tell me you had something figured out

Well I did test one button juice has a high pH if we added lemon juice it'd cut the basicity to neutral I believe it would taste better

let me tell you after that trip with Lucy and Sally I need something I mean you try a week with two girls twenty-four hours a day real sensitive no genital sex trying to dig and build good emotional moods you'd feel a strain too

I can imagine

Not that I didn't love it should've been with us when we hit Monument Valley there'd just been a cloud burst white clouds over about half the sky they would've been white that is but they were red from reflecting the sandstone so anyway we had that whole canyon road to ourselves because it was cut out in a few places Lucy got a little worried about her new Chevvy anyway the damndest thing on those sand dunes we heard some bells I looked up and saw a Navajo sheep dog and I started to bark playing you know but Sally cried look look she really took to the West after this happened by the way let down her long hair played her flute for us she's a funny one she always envies Fran and Lucy their accomplishments and nerve but she organizes socialist/civil rights meetings smokes pot plays the flute digs

Vivaldi Scarlatti works every summer and at school for almost every cent she'd got anyway behind this dog another and maybe forty sheep two or three of them black and five or six goats I said now the little Navajo girl will come

Yeah I can see it

Yeah only the Navajo girl didn't show

A troop of Navajos on horses

No nobody showed Lucy Sally and I drew together no humans and these animals continued over the sand dunes you know it's at least a mile over that pure sand from one valley to the other

Yeah

Well the animals were moving out over that sand under those red cliffs from one valley to the other one of them or more had decided to change valleys and they'd set off

Maybe the Navajos were behind a ways

No after they passed by the sand dunes where we stood we ran down to the car and drove to a high point and watched them a long time I don't believe Lucy even took any pictures they just kept moving across that sand silent and animal almost like they didn't need us sheep goats and dogs of course they do

Of course

Then on top of the Grand Canyon I saw a red mushroom

I know the kind you mean a big one with a growth about half way up on the stem

Yes with gills underneath I was on my early morning walk I thought I have to wake Lucy and Sally up to see it they rubbed eyes and stretched Sally stretched real funny she sits up legs straight out in the sleeping bag and stretched from the waist wiggling her fingers in the sky on the way to the mushroom a big Muley buck promenaded parallel with us about forty yards away through the yellow pines Lucy got a real bang out of that we reached the mushroom it still had dirt spots on the crown it'd pushed up so fast I lay down on my stomach before it I couldn't move Sally did the same Lucy began taking pictures of me us it from every angle I couldn't even get angry or amused I reached out my finger and diddled the cool moist gills the red crude vigorous crown hypnotized me like it removed me from the world of time

Sounds like a great trip

Bill the thing is I stopped by my folks for a day on the way back I still didn't tell them I'm going to quit it all I've got to give notice to Worldwide pretty quick too

Saves a lot of fuss to wait till last minute

Yeah I'm just going to write them well I'm taking off and then ignore the shock and unbelief letters

They never learn do they my folks still unbelieved when I came to the village

Bill how about the peyote

Okay we've got to do something for the taste though

Three weeks

Alright

What about the Adirondacks

Alright I know a spot

I feel like more every day I can really let myself go I'm really eager to see what happens this time

I hope I can let go too

Hell you're bound to

I want to pick out a good girl this time though I mean one whom I can trust

It'll work out Bill you know it almost seems my whole life since I was eighteen's been a waste I'd quit college I'd worked around since I was fourteen I was reading Jung and Dostoyevsky on the San Francisco waterfront working at odd jobs Blake Neitszche Whitman Shaxpere Joyce in my blood who'd believe all the rest it'll sound megalomaniac but I was where Rimbaud was at eighteen and I let the bastards wave another scholarship under my nose I was incredulous I'd said fuck it all and fought it out with my folks what made me go back I remember he said well you can write at Railroad Son's University and there you don't have to work the scholarship pays I said I hate required courses he said you take what you want long as the professor OK's you I said hell there's only five days left before classes you need to register months before, he said no we always save a spot for someone like you I weakened Bill how I sold out I said Okay but maybe I'll quit in a quarter he said try it and we'll see

You quit though didn't you

Sure after one quarter I could only stand two classes one on writing one on medieval history I wrote on total recall story old Bailey wrote you have mental diarrhea she was great the next I did straight realism she said exciting as describing going up a thirty-nine steps staircase by saying he stepped on the first step he stepped on the second step the funny thing I told her I'm quitting she said first I want you to see an important literary agent/critic in San Francisco you should get a first rate man's opinion I'll ask him to read whatever you bring you know I've never told anyone this before Bill he had a large swanky apartment with what I thought then was an English accent but it may have only been a Harvard one tall a little frail English sportcoat books and art objects everywhere distrusted him and at the same time waited with awe for his pronouncement just to see what someone oracular could possibly say he finally finished I pulled out his Finnegan's Wake copy and browsed while he read my sheets he finally said I don't think I can make any really valuable specific criticisms then he pointed to a few phrases the main mission which I have to perform he finally said is to assure you that you will/or should become an important writer

What's wrong with that

An important writer I hated importance it sounded in my ears like institutions prisons coteries and yet I never forgot it I went down to a border town ate oranges sugarcane joints meat they pulled ripping deep up to the hairy forearms out of fly infested bowls and tired out whores I loved their cheap pictures of the Virgin Mary and they're all different human variety is endless and wrote madly two hundred pages which I hitchhiked back across the country with to have Bill Appleby my best friend at the college I'd quit read it. He even started typing it up he became overworked anyhow he seemed to lose interest about page one hundred. I thought what the hell I need to try again learn more I took up left wing politics engineering science administration the whole bit all of this a lie I always want to find a meaning and I always seem to think of meaning in terms of a pattern I could weave you myth after myth

it's something to have lived a legend

here's the latest one a la Joyce at nineteen they caught me my religion democracy my countrymen the oppressed my language revolt but I failed to attain to wholeness harmony radiance though I tried first lyrical self-expression then plunged into mediate state of participating in epic searches and finally with Worldwide pared my fingernails and with Rufus Brown contemplated Godlike the drama of the world but now I'll fly on a Yugoslav freighter they'll never catch me again.

That's a good one that what you really think

I think everything I hate thinking I love thinking the most amoral free glorious gift of life if you include logic imagination intuition the whole array of conscious skills but it dies with the coagulating and rotting blood it serves the cunning not-to-be suppressed sperm and belly sometimes I think the universe runs riot in me and I'm tired of governing supposing I say all power to the mob to the anarchists to every red flag in every gland storm me smash the barricades drag me out of all police stations factories drawing rooms offices laboratories shout and fulfill your every secret wish all power possible to every autonomous soviet of my present fictitious knout and whip Czarist unification I am a prisonhouse of souls

37

Three weeks later I was cowering in grey September drizzle just clearing off, chilled, a hundred feet from a small cabin whose window shone yellow, the only light around except the stars, inside Bill Layton his girl of the past month and mine Lita Chayevsky. I'm certain Bill will shoot me down if I advance to the door Lita's gone in to check the situation out it had all started off badly I wrote Fran now back in the States but we hadn't seen each other let's go to the Adirondacks have peyote and talk she'd written me to come to New England to see her for a talk she wrote back how after all that's between us could you expect us to spend a weekend in such a manner and such a place on a just-friends basis well let's let what happens happen I wrote back Let me make it clearer she replied I don't want to so stormy artist Lita and I up together she very nervous but determined Bill's girl a nurse frightened of taking anything in her system but wanting to loosen up same as him I seemed to be pushing everybody that's very bad but somehow I had to try it again we'd hiked around a canyon but all day drizzly the leaves still faded green with late summer autumn color not really started we'd driven long and hard from New York City because Lita had to work till midnight saving money for her European trip we'd not over four hours sleep we sat around the iron stove fire stoked up even that seemed not very cheery it wasn't in a good open fireplace you had to pull, open a metal door for even a small view Bill said over and over God the stuff tastes like shit I hate to think of taking it again his girl giggled nervously Lita looked at me I knew she had not the strongest stomach and Doris with great constitution had thrownup I said repeating what Bill had first told me a year ago well it's just the opposite of alcohol all the bad effects are in the beginning no hangover anyhow and this lemon juice might help

the stuff must be taken in happy surroundings and with everyone trusting Bill and I said this over and over but here I was pushing look I said it's almost sunset if we want any color at all we have to start after it was all prepared and poured standing in four tall glasses no one seemed to want to drink Bill had even gotten my stomach queasy the stuff *is* lousy finally we all got it down

I turned on in about two mintues I don't believe it said Lita she and I had this running fight she was certain I was a fake, Russian Jewish gold ear-ringed nineteen she wore no bra she talked a tremendous sex game but she always said why can't I stop thinking I just keep thinking thinking and sometimes it even seems disgusting she painted sturdy choppy lines and strokes I burst outside I looked at a leaf's inside valley not just water but twenty-one separate drops gleaming crystalline touching the leaf only on the bottom of a curled-up ball I counted them they each seemed unique placing my forefinger carefully at the leaf's tip I arced them one by one off the leaf and down among the blades of grass where they splashed and broke flicking little bits of color

down on my knees my fingers plunged into the ground my fuck-you finger stroke one grass root a tight wire balancer on steel and sprayed aside the dirt following its nether course plucking it a guitar string from time to time it never broke nuzzled my head against Lita's knee oh goody I always wanted Joe to be a dog for me

Bill rose alert a deer breaking brush there she is he said and pointed toward the woods I snaked on my belly toward it Lita ran dancing in front of me I snaked to her so fast she couldn't dodge caught her ankle and brought her down.

Bill and his girl went inside Lita and I followed

The embers swelled sank red glow flaring in out everything quiet Bill and his girl then Lita then myself furthest from the stove I felt restless lonely Bill and his girl absorbed in each other and the embers nobody said anything let's go outside I whispered to Lita loud enough for Bill to hear let's get out of this cabin outside it'll be splendid

She shook her head longer silence unbearable

Goodbye I said at the door I glanced back no one looked at me they lay three logs parallel to the stove I wished Bill would get up and come with me but not a motion soft snapples crackles I tried to open and close the door without a sound

I hated to walk with every step I felt the powerful pointed blades meet the boot sole head-on their splintering apart forcing down in all directions cracking and sundering of drier parts under the punishment

my lips wriggling they formed shape after shape exquisitely flexible they rotted so easily they sucked under each other twisted side to side folded and broke folds sent waves pulsing from corner to corner, above me white white white the Milky Way contempt and pity for the yellow-red light from the cabin window the three lying inside like cordwood my whole body undulated except my spine remained straight flesh the other bones moved crawled danced Universe you rot not only lips but bones dance itself dies out I cried each word slowly in stentorian whispers toward beyond the stars the great blackness in the white white white focused my vision astronomers call you stellar dust no you are nothing death from beyond the stars someday all the stars eaten only the black remains not empty black black death alive insatiable starving all will be eaten death will starve to death

A tail grew down from behind cold I shivered I could not go back inside they lay there huddling imagine themselves a center of universe billions of them small houses/caves inside huddling people/animals outside wolves prowled they did ever imagine what prowled around their windows, looked imagined laughed wept raided fled and behind us the shivering wolves circling and looking in the billion homes the billion stars each lonely/lost and through them eating or maybe not eat just absorbing glopping death

Well better wolf if that's what I really am better starving shivering outcast anything better than huddling to another scared illusion

Jo-o-o-e Jo-o-o-e

I slowly danced my way around the cabin

Jo-o-o-e   Lost forlorn resonant

Lita walked out in the open space

Here I caught her hand we looked at each other her eyes wide open

I was so frightened in there they didn't want me the longer I stayed the more they turned against me they didn't say anything I felt it hate washed out against me I don't know what I'd do if I hadn't found you

I shushed her finger to my lip hand on her waist I began swaying

I never knew you could move like that

I can't I'm a wolf

to slight finger pressures she began swaying her large eyes seeming frightened followed my face they couldn't leave I couldn't stand it I danced away and across the grass her eyes never left me I did every motion for her

I wish Bill'd come out with us I said

I don't think he will I think he wants to

We whispered to each other wide-eyed

She's not taking it very well is she

no I think he's taking care of her he's so tender

He should let her alone he should be out here with us

She's so frightened

I think she will always be frightened Bill needs this

let's try to get them out

We tried they wouldn't come they lay like two strangers holding each other they didn't hardly look at us except once in a while to stare I feel the hate too I whispered very very low to Lita

Outside again I was shaking you know Bill's my brother but I think he'd shoot me now I think he'd stand on that porch and shoot me a shivering wolf down I felt murder in his soul I felt we'd become two different things that nothing now exists between us

No she murmured you and he love each other it'll be better tomorrow it's this stuff it's frightening

He will cling to her nothing will ever make him leave I am a wolf I face the death beyond the stars I look longingly at his comfort his fire but I am not of that we are different essences

No no no

I cannot go in we will sleep in the car I'm sorry it's very cold but I cannot go in he should come out in the world of stars and death listen to the waves

chittering liquid rustling the leaves of the forest like ocean waves like onslapping rivers forever same forever different sounds, limitless, impelled by something beyond and within us all, the gods stand around us tonight I ran from her by the edge on the forest rain and ran peering up through chittering liquid sounds trees dark dark down low, light dark above, stars at intervals shining through, warm friendly close beneficient stars part of our world part of our warmth the stars lost fires of separated fellows. The gods just inside the forest embittered from inside the leaves. Marsala at the pueblo really felt them and now I really felt them. The gods ran freely as I in the forests they bathed in mountain streams they too died from death beyond the stars

the gods live the gods live why doesn't Bill come out

You must go in talk with him

I'm frightened he'll shoot me down he'll not see the gods he'll see the grey cold shivering wolf

You must try

We've reached it nothing's eternal not even brotherhood

You can't given that up you have to try

her eyes wide tragic fears Fran Lucy Rufus she was right not to try was tragic I had to try

You go first make sure he wants me in at all

She disappeared small pert brave I shivered in the increasing cold.

Come in she finally called. Inside the lights all on noise clatter Bill stood in the door of the kitchen chewing coarsely crudely his girl behind him as if frightened of me I knew it I knew they'd see the wolf even Lita stared at me they were surrounding me warmth lights food blankets they'd trap me want something to eat Bill smiled rip off that fucking mask you're scared to face it and you want me to eat to become part of this lie no no I stiffened

I came to talk to you of the gods and you have offered me soup

I know he said both smiling and sad ah he realizes what he is doing and still he does it

I turned and strode out Lita could stay or come as she damn pleased.

38

Lita and I stood about forty feet from the cabin door

I'm cold she said

I'm cold too

Let's go in

No he refused to come out he doesn't want us

We can't freeze all night

Let's wait till they go to bed we'll sneak in

We stood arm in arm sides pressed against each other this stuff makes you so sensitive she said I don't think I like it the way I felt their hate for me the way you and Bill aren't understanding

You'd prefer lies why was she weakening she'd come out of the cabin so brave did no one prefer exaltation to safety

She screamed

What is it what is it I drew her to me looking around fog flared through the open space white misty everything different somehow

The moon the moon it nearly bit my head off I looked over there and it nearly bit my head off

Above a dark hilltop the reddest bloodiest moon hugest bloodiest moon I ever saw raising its white fangs from out of the hilltop the white mist fled down the open space from its huge red bloody obscene casting light now a dim white bloody light everywhere stars fleeing from it

Lets go in I said we've gone far enough firm definite tone I looked for her grateful look cavalry to the rescue my god Lita all my body melted below my ribs it simply sank away no solid ground Lita her face bones a skull no flesh sockets white white except the socket darks the nose dark the mouth dark all white Lita you're a death's head I pushed her from me I couldn't hold her

Why'd you push me hold me hold me I'm scared

Only mental, pull that to you, pull that to you, her head my fingers just in dry fluffy material she had lost her hair everything dry large feathers black feathers headdress above the pasty white I pushed her away again

Joe what's wrong she screamed I'm scared you push me away

Lita wide tragic eyes small thin-armed before me pleading I drew her to me we've got to go in

Yes yes

In bed we lay her skin exquisite velvet let's don't fuck it'd be a rape now everything's so sensitive

Yes she said

That warm moist mystery always tense about, curious worshipper of, repelled by, vagina cunt mother-channel world-creator hole pisser bleeder lubricant secreter home lover ecstasy reproach I relaxed my finger dallied juicy thick molasses stirring warm thick molasses something hard round coming to an end a soft segmented ridge pet and pet again its segments seemed to trail after departing fingertip such response at the opposite end stretch intriguing a second finger slowly stretch a third no more slowly revolve one way the other way no opposition at the furthest finger tip what goodies on beyond sweet deprivation all cannot be known yet so much

I love you I said

Maybe it wouldn't be too much of a rape she said

Maybe no she stroked me but I curiously felt a cork bobbed on a wrinkling string absolutely relaxed except a slight tension am I spoiling it for her

I never felt so complete I said

Why don't you try to write something of what you feel

What an effort

No you're really having an experience try I'll draw something

She crouched naked before her drawing pad then made lines with her pen she'd never show me I wrote a few words and then I sketched outlines of her crouching her head bent forward between her calves her arm coming down her side reaching around her ankle her knees the highest part of her above the floor she made motions absorbed as a child

Late the next night Bill said he just didn't get anything out of it

39 The freighter finally sailed actually propellored out nosed along by two tugs on a cold midnight in mid-November as we slid along under the span of Verrazano bridge I thought it'll be completed and all Staten Island changed before I return what won't be though I'd seen Fran two days previous the proximate cause having been the delay for the freighter for an extra two days the effective cause that we both wanted to since she had returned from Europe but terms and conditions never quite satisfactory to either, this one time she'd came down to New York I'd had to be out West on the geology bit. I enjoyed that, turnabout's fair play since she wouldn't come to the Adirondacks but now sailing in two days nothing could really happen to involve us we could let go I called her long distance the truth is the second time I called her since once at end of September I had but she not in we'd both kept touch through Sally now back from San Francisco who gently prodded also for us to talk the final cause who knows

Joe she said that warm clear slightly high voice she sang soprano not a touch of the affected free of all taint of whine and nasal affecting most American women none of the jaw rumble of the British nor lost R's of Harvard her speech flowed deep pools white rapids no throat constrictions or rasps a slight aspirant enthusiasm gleaming exquisitely surfaces of that limpidity

Yeah I'm leaving the States in two days I'd like to come up to see you this afternoon and tomorrow

I want to see you

Yeah well I'll be there about three

The train rolled along the Hudson bankruptcies vision greed coal diesel union with the Midwest Chicago Vanderbilt Jay Gould strikes of '77 and '86 Manifest Destiny I leaned back on the soiled worn blue seat pretty decrepit in its old age rectangular deserted boarding houses here and there rusty siding stops long abandoned imagine Henry with his sails upon that river over three hundred years old how long can one excuse with "Young" Isfahan is younger and so is Petro-Leningrad

Moved with the taxi hermetic from all life of the industrial town except it uncoordinated traffic lights, on the taxi radio an exasperated girl's voice asking locations giving addresses and routes trying to optimize movements of twenty cabs few people on the streets they dashed from car into a store back to car and into home, we've deserted our streets desolation's triumph, a girl stares at me out the side window of a car we pass, I stare desperately back our machines pull us apart

I wait in the dormitory lobby maybe we will hug and kiss will we stare

Tall she advances down the corridor it's too much for me the moment rushes by her hand's shaking mine mutter something we're outside look laugh we stride along vigorously cool sun grey clouds tall century old trees spaces about the campus

You want to go see a cider mill

Sure

We take off walking and walking houses disappear dairy cattle grazing tilted limestone exposures in the road cuts we buy apples at the cider mill let's come back tonight to eat, fine, her cheeks glow red no rouge blood under the translucency she waves at two friends bicycling by the city has surrounded us new houses appear an arc of four lane superhighway, frontier's only in art and we head out path ending or a brickglass factory, stroll to the end of their gravel drive.

Why did you stop loving me Fran you told me that you loved me and loved me why did you stop

We sat down on the gravel she in her plain grey skirt and locked her hands in front of her close together uprisen knees

that train argument that couldn't have been all of it everyone has arguments not so drastic some but more others

but I don't want such deep tearing arguments

Fran if you have deep movings toward you'll also have deep movings against at least I do

I want to build the subtle finer threads the slow long continuing growth

Words words I grew desperate have to talk with her

You never wanted me to see your family again

Why not good enough or you not strong enough

You were/are different I wanted both but not together I didn't want either spoiled the other separate it had to be

You always brag of your tradition don't you think I have any

No at least different from mine you come roaring intensity moment chaos

You talked of your piano your singing your Grandfather's traditions we had Christmas dinner forty of us the women cooked cleaned cared for the children talked cajoled and sympathized the men went for walks studying wheat and cattle you and I both come from the same tradition

No how

Your people stayed behind but both yours and mine they came here looking for something yours found and stayed here mine never found it they always moved West yet you're still looking your Grandfather gave up his banking for science and FDR all people everywhere look we are searchers Fran that's the oldest best tradition but my people too as well as yours knew how to revel by the winter fire-side

I like the way you're talking so quietly now

Fran you were a lovely fuck

I was so scared you'd be one of those you can't talk afterwards

Why I always like to stay friends it's with girls it's hard to do

Men too she laughed

Impulses impulses Fran perhaps we should marry what a conjoining of forces together we span our country

No it can never be

You loved me you know you did

As if a sphere inside me revolved it had held you in its light but it revolved I didn't do it just happened and that's now dark and it lights another

You really love another

Yes not the same way what can ever be the same it's what I want in some ways I'm doing more daring things than with you only now I don't wage great open struggles with my family I do them secretly

You shouldn't have told them they wrote me bitter letters telephoned threats

I believed in honesty full open disclosures I hadn't learned

people in suits popped out of the industrial building glanced at us briefly entered their cars and drove away the day colder the gravel we sat on hard I reached for the hand of the glowing grey-eyed white head-banded woman

We skipped and strode back along the road

Let's try a different way she said

Corn stalks weathering streaky grey askew in a field of clods a line of trees on the far side outlined a streams course over the suburban houses west of the farm course chalky red alternated with clouds

We had spear fights with those we pulled them out dirt stuck to the roots a great blunt point we hurled them at each other

She laughed excited

And clod fights and rock fights only they weren't fair and snowball fights only you weren't supposed to soak them in water we looked at the sky at a branch above us at a twig at the furthest twig bent and black at that twig against the darkening sky

St Catherine of Teresa I said after a while likened humanity to twigs and branches we can never know each other by trying to meet twig to twig we are unutterably separate but if we go deep inside ourselves down to the very roots we mingle one with all our brothers/sisters

We finally turned from the twig and hiked down the ruts that ran by the trees between us and the stream course is there a bridge down there?

I don't know maybe we'd better turn back

There's bound to be a way this is the built-up East

Finally we struck off down through the trees a stream about eight feet across cut us off on down we saw houses again

I know there's a bridge on the other side of those houses she said

Let's try here we looked for a narrow place there wasn't any

Let's go back she said

A fury overtook me no no I looked around I would lose I would be betrayed if we retreated

A fallen tree about eight inches in diameter behind us My hands seized it stand back I couldn't do it too heavy must do it my back trembled my arms trembled raising it aloft ran three steps launched it a pathway across wild exultant I broke a small rotten trunk and poled it down into the muddy bottom athwart my bridge for piling.

I reached my hand out as she followed after we stumbled our way through dark wet grass thistles and burrs pulled at us I tried to pick a good way we made it to the road I wanted to dance kinesthesia

That night we drank hot cider and ate thick oatmeal cookies at the cider mill then continued to the college 3.2 beer hall juke box and danceplace Fran sat down on the floor right in front of the fire we stared into the flicker/flare/heat until my face seemed burnt and my crossed legs ached we talked of many things and many silences put parks between

Remember Chartres I said

She nodded she'd finally talked me into going

We'd looked around and around it an old American about seventy sat in a pew seat with binoculars we avoided him ashamed of our provincial own full of my knowledge of history your knowledge of esthetics we walked around and reveled in our brilliance meeting a cathedral worthy of it all

Just before we left we stopped for a last summing-up look near the old man Want to use these binoculars you can see some interesting things with them now you take that legend of Saint Matthew depicted yonder

Enthralled alternating with the binoculars we followed his finger around the immense vault

You see he said I built highways and railroads all over New Mexico and Arizona and Nevada I think I kind of understood these old boys they were builders but they had a special faith I suppose till they invented binoculars nobody could even appreciate it I mean people could sit down here and they could never see that detail I pointed out to you and they thought nobody would ever see it but that didn't matter to them because to them it was for Mary mother of God they did it we'd go and invent binoculars and spy out that they'd never cheated but given full measure and beyond that even

We handed him back his binoculars

Thank you

Oh it's not much I retired two years ago my wife and I went to England to see the place we came from kind of a long time ago but then I guess before that everybody in the world all came from the same place I reckon they thought I was too old to build for them in New Mexico and Arizona any more anyhow I started looking at these old cathedrals and got right carried away my wife thinks I'm a little batty about them but I seem to see something in them so I'm wandering about looking at a few

Remember the third class Spanish train

Remember

Remember

Remember

We held hands before the fire

The next day she cut classes we talked for hours

You're doing the right thing you're equipped as few have ever been to observe the world you always observe don't you

I participate I

Yes but somewhere you're always the observer even on our great train fight you were observing I bet you could play it all back you were born it seems to me with a kind of detachment I don't mean you don't care you do but as if you are always able to see what you are doing

I wish I didn't a lot of the time when I come back we'll talk again

Oh yes we must always from time to time talk

If I write a book I ought to dedicate it to you and Rufus Brown

Why don't you

Well it'd really have to be to all those who've nudged me but you and Rufus certainly have been special

What did I want what would/could the world give for what I gave I wanted everything that it would give I wanted to press it beyond would to could but Fran and I had finished talking no plots no ends in this world our only world get while the getting's good leave while the going's good give/take what you can blackness sunshine blood brain cold warm

A One

So long I said
So long
Almost had to leave without you the busdriver joshed
Yeah the freighter waited in the Brooklyn jungle Africa Asia my soul my book life death awaited Yeah I almost got carried away almost forgot to wave for you to stop.

A Two

My fingers skittered and squeaked off the windows
sliding down the all glass skyscraper impenetrable
though translucent busy life inside the building building even as I fall and see

A Three

On top the dome glacial ice cirques and crags timberline fringed by gnarled storm-flattened distorted pines at each side a wapiti stag antlered head high listening to far winds each eye a wolf black grizzled grey white-fanged and tawney-eyed each cheek a bactrian camel marching through drought and famine the nose twisting tendriled at bottom furling up heavy white petals in their center black stamens lulling with gravid odors lips a cobra and rattle-snake intertwined from the aperture issues forth a waterfall over the bulrush and bamboo chin all floating on a bog of mud

They ain't no end
But here I stop
Adios friend/foe/brother/sister